PENGUIN CLASSICS

# THE SAGA OF KING HROLF KRAKI

Written by an anonymous author in fourteenth-century Iceland, *The Saga of King Hrolf Kraki* is built on almost a thousand years of oral traditions, many of which are related to underlying stories found in the Anglo-Saxon epic Beowulf.

Reaching into the mists of Scandinavia's most ancient history, *Hrolf's Saga* tells of events set in the Migration Period when warrior chieftains and their proud women ruled, loved and feuded in the northern lands.

JESSE L. BYOCK is Professor of Old Norse and Medieval Scandinavian at the University of California, Los Angeles, and a member of the UCLA's Institute of Archaeology. He has published numerous articles and books on Iceland and the Sagas, including *Medieval Iceland: Society, Sagas and Power, Feud in the Icelandic Saga* and a translation of *The Saga of the Volsungs: The Norse Epic of Sigurd the Dragon Slayer*. Professor Byock received his Ph.D. from Harvard University after studying in Iceland, Sweden and France. A specialist in North Atlantic and Viking studies, his work has been supported by grants from the National Endowment for the Humanities, the Fulbright Foundation and the John Simon Guggenheim Foundation.

# THE SAGA OF
# KING HROLF KRAKI

*Translated with an introduction by*
JESSE L. BYOCK

PENGUIN BOOKS

PENGUIN BOOKS

Published by the Penguin Group
Penguin Books Ltd, 80 Strand, London WC2R 0RL, England
Penguin Putnam Inc., 375 Hudson Street, New York, New York 10014, USA
Penguin Books Australia Ltd, 250 Camberwell Road, Camberwell, Victoria 3124, Australia
Penguin Books Canada Ltd, 10 Alcorn Avenue, Toronto, Ontario, Canada M4V 3B2
Penguin Books India (P) Ltd, 11 Community Centre, Panchsheel Park, New Delhi – 110 017, India
Penguin Books (NZ) Ltd, Cnr Rosedale and Airborne Roads, Albany, Auckland, New Zealand
Penguin Books (South Africa) (Pty) Ltd, 24 Sturdee Avenue, Rosebank 2196, South Africa

Penguin Books Ltd, Registered Offices: 80 Strand, London WC2R 0RL, England

www.penguin.com

First published 1998

029

Copyright © Jesse L. Byock, 1998
All rights reserved

The moral right of the translator has been asserted

Set in 10/12.5 pt Monotype Bembo
Typeset by Rowland Phototypesetting Ltd, Bury St Edmunds, Suffolk
Printed and bound in Great Britain by Clays Ltd, Elcograf S.p.A.

ISBN-13: 978-0-141-43593-1

www.greenpenguin.co.uk

MIX
Paper from
responsible sources
FSC® C018179

Penguin Books is committed to a sustainable
future for our business, our readers and our planet.
This book is made from Forest Stewardship
Council™ certified paper.

# Contents

## THE SAGA

v

# Introduction

*The Saga of King Hrolf Kraki* is one of the major Scandinavian legendary tales and belongs to the group of mythic – heroic Icelandic stories known as the 'sagas of ancient times', or *fornaldar* sagas. These texts, which are also sometimes called the 'legendary sagas', are distinctive in that they tell of events that occurred, or are supposed to have occurred, long before the ninth-century settlement of Iceland. A narrative about pre-Viking Age kings and their rivals, *Hrolf's Saga*, as the text is often called, tells of King Hrolf, a warrior chieftain who ruled in Denmark in about the sixth century AD. Called Kraki (tall, angular and slender like a pole ladder), Hrolf was widely remembered in the medieval North as one of the most magnificent kings of 'ancient times', and the saga draws on a long oral tradition as it describes Hrolf's often treacherous family and recounts the exploits of his famous champions.

*Hrolf's Saga*, which was written in prose in fourteenth-century Iceland, has close affinities with the Old English verse epic *Beowulf*, written sometime in the period from the eighth to the early eleventh centuries. Both compositions draw on a common tradition of storytelling, recounting events that may or may not have occurred in the fifth- and/or sixth-century Danish kingdom of the Skjoldungs (Old English: *Scyldinga*). And both, though differentiated by centuries of independent transmission in different lands, have many of the same characters and settings. The relationship is based on an ancient core of shared storytelling, which displays the extent of a common oral tradition in the medieval North and may echo long-past historical events. *Hrolf's Saga* and *Beowulf* share a further similarity. Each provides information about a powerful champion whose bearlike character may reflect the distant memory of early cultic practices.

Medieval Iceland was a suitable place for passing down the memory of King Hrolf and his twelve champions. The settlement of Iceland, an island country first colonized by Norsemen in the ninth century, was an offshoot of Viking Age (c. 800–1070) exploration and westward expansion across the North Atlantic. At considerable distance from Europe, Iceland was a frontier country. As in such communities elsewhere, the settlers and their descendants tended to venerate the traditions of the mother-culture. The Icelanders' knowledge of the Scandinavian past was so broad that in medieval times they were acknowledged throughout the North to be master storytellers and the keepers of ancient poetic lore. The Danish historian Saxo Grammaticus, writing about 1200, credits the trustworthiness of Icelanders, who:

spend their time improving knowledge of others' deeds, making up for their poverty by their intelligence. They take great pleasure in discovering and commemorating the achievements of all nations; in their view it is as enlightening to discourse on the prowess of others as to display their own.

In recounting their own past and the history of other peoples, Icelandic saga tellers made prose narration a high art. Their sagas were unusual among the literatures of medieval Europe where, with the exception of Ireland, traditional narrative stories were usually told in verse. The introduction in Iceland of the written saga in the twelfth century invigorated the process of narrative innovation. Writing provided Icelandic saga tellers with broader possibilities for reworking and preserving the lore of the past. In the case of the legends surrounding King Hrolf and his retinue of champions, the saga tellers had at their disposal an extensive body of existing heroic lore.

The various stories concerning Hrolf and his heroes were first assembled in a coherent, single text possibly as early as the thirteenth century. In its present form, *Hrolf's Saga* was composed around 1400. In 1461 a copy of a saga about Hrolf was included among the 'books in the Norse language' in the library of the monastery of Modruvellir in northern Iceland. Today the earliest of the forty-four known manuscripts dates from the seventeenth century, and all of these are copies deriving ultimately from a single common ancestor. The saga author, well aware that he was arranging a compilation of older material, retains the episodic structure of his sources, often telling the audience when one sub-tale ends and another begins: 'Here ends the tale of Frodi and now begins the story of Hroar and Helgi, the sons of Halfdan.'

If the underlying, individual episodes are often discernible, the saga is, nevertheless, a unified work, very much in the matter-of-fact style of the Icelandic family sagas. Even in the passages that treat fabulous events and creatures, the text uses an understated tone, relying on realistic-sounding description to create an almost believable story. So too the physical world of the saga is presented in non-fabulous geographical terms, and one can place most events on a modern map. Centred on the court at Hleidargard (Old Norse *Hleidr*, modern Danish Lejre) on the island of Sjaelland, the action spreads across the legendary landscape of northern Europe from Lapland in the far north to England in the west.

Because the saga, like many medieval tales, is fashioned from disparate parts, it is helpful to keep the basic structure in mind. The text falls into five main sections, each one focusing on a different set of characters. The common connection with Hrolf, the male and female members of his family, and his court unites the episodes, giving the saga a consistent narrative focus. The first section (chaps. 1–4) gives the often modest Hrolf an illustrious pedigree. Opening with a dynastic conflict, the saga plunges into the struggle between King Halfdan and his brother Frodi, who were greatly dissimilar in character. At issue was control of the Danish kingdom. In this first part the saga teller uses the unfolding conflict to introduce Hrolf's tempestuous ancestors. These include the young princes; Helgi, Hrolf's father; Hroar, his uncle; and Signy, his aunt.

The second section (chaps. 5–13) traces events in the lives of Helgi and Hroar. In particular, the narrative at this point follows the actions of Helgi, a man with large and sometimes uncontrollable appetites. Despite the fact that on each occasion the women caution him not to act on his impulse, Helgi plunges into a series of unfortunate sexual liaisons. The stories of the women then enter the tale, and here we first meet Hrolf's mother Yrsa, a person of uncommon heritage. The events of Yrsa's life, including her marriages and wishes, form a narrative thread, linking different sections of the saga and touching the lives of many of the characters. Toward the end of the second section King Hrolf is born, the offspring of a curious parentage. In the next section (chaps. 14–16) the saga turns to Hrolf's champions, explaining how the Swede Svipdag battles the berserkers of King Adils of Sweden before coming into King Hrolf's service.

The fourth section (chaps. 16–24) takes the tale to Norway and Lapland and is one of the saga's episodic gems. Virtually a fully formed tale in itself, it recounts the fate of Bjorn, the 'man–bear'. This tragic tale of ancient magic offers insight into the supernatural gifts of Bjorn's sons, including the bearlike nature of Bodvar Bjarki. A sword hidden in a cave and embedded in stone awaits the rightful heir among Bjorn's three sons. In this section each occurrence is more extraordinary than the preceding one. Not the least of these is the shield wall constructed of bones with its occupant Hjalti, the champion who confronts and conquers fear.

Up to this point Hrolf himself plays a relatively minor role in the saga. Like Charlemagne in the sequence of Norse stories named after him or like Arthur in medieval Romance tradition, Hrolf the great king of the North is often overshadowed by the individual stories about his champions. With all the pieces in place, however, the fifth and last part of the saga (chaps. 24–34) concentrates on King Hrolf himself and his unfolding destiny. The retinue of champions has reached its full strength, and the central female characters have been introduced into the saga. In the Scandinavian dynastic struggles that form the major underlying theme in the rest of the saga, King Adils of Sweden emerges as Hrolf's principal opponent. Here both Bodvar Bjarki and the god Odin (in the guise of Hrani) play crucial, though very different, roles.

*Hrolf's Saga* devotes a significant share of the narrative to the destiny of female characters, and a significant feature of the text is that important events turn on decisions made by women. Queens, sorceresses, a freeman's loyal daughter and an elfin woman and her daughter all change the destiny of those who encounter them. Kings and jarls (earls) frequently seek the advice of the women, and the intimate details of marriages, whether good or bad, are exposed. This emphasis is possible because a number of prominent male heroes in *Hrolf's Saga* are only marginally involved in stories of maturation, whereby a boy, such as

Sigurd in *The Saga of the Volsungs*, comes of age. According to the basic maturation story, a 'helper' or 'donor' assists the boy in acquiring special weapons and/or knowledge. The youth uses these acquisitions to prove himself through deeds, finding in the end a bride and thereby consummating the transition to manhood. To be sure, elements of this traditional pattern are found in *Hrolf's Saga*, as for instance in the intertwined stories of Bodvar Bjarki and Hjalti. In the main, however, *Hrolf's Saga*, like *Beowulf*, is about mature people. The action concentrates on adults such as Queen Yrsa and her husbands, King Helgi and King Adils, and the saga probes deeply into the often complex emotional and sexual needs of such individuals.

While King Hrolf remains the central focus, it is frequently the women who connect the saga's different episodes, binding the individual pieces of story into a cohesive whole. Consider Queen Yrsa: she first enters the tale as an impoverished child of uncertain birth. Taken captive at an early age, Yrsa is forced to marry King Helgi. Against the odds, the union is good; she comes to love Helgi and he her. The ramifications of this love and the psychological unease caused by the abrupt termination of the marriage, affect the lives of almost all of the saga's subsequent characters. And what a story it is. Yrsa, forced by conventions of morality, throws her happiness away and as a grown woman returns to live with Queen Olof, the mother who hates her. From this point on, Yrsa's life is a dilemma. Her previous husband, King Helgi, remains in love with her. But Helgi, although normally a forceful man, becomes immobilized, his heart broken. In what we now would understand as a deep depression, Helgi retires to his bed. Yrsa, too, suffers cruelly. Her only route of escape from Queen Olof is marriage to King Adils of Sweden, a man whom she dislikes. From Yrsa's second forced marriage will come her greatest loss.

Queen Yrsa does not employ magic, but many of the other women of the saga do. Queen White, the Lapp king's daughter, Heid, the seeress, and Queen Skuld all find empowerment in magic and sorcery. Skuld, the enigmatic half-elfin woman, proves to be a fearful opponent, conjuring up among other feats a monstrous boar. Men in the saga also utilize magic as we see in the behaviour of Vifil the commoner, the warrior Bodvar Bjarki and King Adils. The example of these characters makes *The Saga of King Hrolf Kraki* a valuable text for understanding the northern perception of magic and sorcery in the late medieval period. The reader wanting more information concerning such subjects is directed to the Explanatory Notes at the end of the book. There I draw distinctions between different types of magic encountered in the saga and discuss the meanings of terms such as wizards, sorcerers and fetches. The endnotes are also designed to assist the reader wanting additional information about the relationship between *Hrolf's Saga* and other medieval Scandinavian and English texts.

## The Sagas of Ancient Times and Heroic Lays

As mentioned, *Hrolf's Saga* belongs to the group of mythic–heroic Icelandic stories known as the 'sagas of ancient times', or *fornaldar* sagas. For the medieval Icelanders themselves, the *fornaldar* sagas were set in the most distant Scandinavian past, a time of myth and legend. Along with the *Saga of the Volsungs*, *Hrolf's Saga* is the best known of these tales of ancient times. These two texts, which are similar in many ways, are major examples of a large genre of storytelling which was popular in medieval Iceland. Both the Volsung story, concerned with Sigurd the dragon slayer and his family, and *Hrolf's Saga* combine legendary, mythic and Romance traditions which were known beyond the shores of Scandinavia. Containing many international folktale motifs, both sagas derive in part from older heroic poetry, and each contains traces of the mythology of the god Odin. Both sagas have a similar social theme: the tragedy of strife among noble kindred. Whereas the *Volsung Saga* tells mostly of deadly rivalries between individuals from different kingdoms tied together by marriage, *Hrolf's Saga* tends to focus more on quarrels among siblings within the Danish royal family. It is perhaps not entirely by chance that the opening conflict in *Hrolf's Saga* involving a royal uncle, mother and nephew triangle (Frodi, his brother Halfdan's wife and Halfdan's avenging sons) reveals a narrative structure reminiscent of that of Shakespeare's *Hamlet*, a story taken from medieval Danish sources.

Although some of the *fornaldar* sagas were written later than the better known family and kings' sagas, many of them preserve the memory of ancient historical events and of the people involved in them. For example, embellished though their stories are with myth and legend, it is probable that the kings mentioned in *Hrolf's Saga*, such as Frodi, Halfdan, Helgi and Hrolf, were historical chieftains, who lived in Denmark during the Migration Period of the fifth and sixth centuries. Long before Iceland's colonization in the ninth century, the names of these kings were carried to England. They were preserved in Anglo-Saxon written sources which may have depended upon oral tradition from northern Europe carried to Britain at the time of the Germanic invasions in the fifth and sixth centuries. Some of these invaders came from Denmark.

The materials that make up *Hrolf's Saga* survived the transition from pagan to Christian society as well as the accompanying shift from oral to written culture. Many of the legends incorporated in the saga were transmitted orally as heroic lays during the Viking Age. We know something about one of these poems, '*The Lay of Bjarki*' (*Bjarkamál*), a heroic lay from the mid-tenth century. Although *Bjarkamál* is no longer fully extant, it is worthwhile to consider the way in which its contents survived independently of *Hrolf's Saga*.

Significant parts of *Bjarkamál* are preserved in the work of Saxo Grammaticus, who translated the lay into Latin hexameters in his *History of the Danes* (*Gesta Danorum*). Of crucial importance is the fact that a few of the lay's verses are quoted in the Old Icelandic by Snorri Sturluson (1179–1241), the powerful Icelandic chieftain and man of letters who inserted the verses into his *Prose Edda* as well as into *Saint Olaf's Saga*. In both instances these originally oral stanzas were incorporated into the written texts because they possessed the timeless power to move audiences, whether pagan or Christian. The heroic deeds of King Hrolf and his champions had long since become a symbol for courage and the prowess of a warrior in medieval Scandinavian culture.

According to Snorri in *Saint Olaf's Saga*, *Bjarkamál* was recited on the morning of the important battle of Stiklestad in 1030. The Christian king of Norway, Saint Olaf, ordered his personal skald, the Icelander Thormod Kolbrun's-poet, to rouse the king's army, inciting it to battle against his pagan foes by reciting the opening verses of *Bjarkamál*. These were the same verses that Bodvar Bjarki was said to have sung at

Hleidargard half a millennium earlier when inciting King Hrolf's warriors to stand firm in their last battle:

> The day has arisen,
> the cock's wings resound.
> Time is for thralls
> to get to their work.
> Awake now, be awake,
> closest of friends,
> all the best
> companions of Adils.

> Har the Hard-griper,
> Hrolf the Bowman,
> good men of noble lineage,
> who never flee.
> I wake you not for wine
> nor for women's mysteries;
> rather I wake you for
> the hard game of war.

## Skjold and the Skjoldung Dynasty: The Legendary Past

Hrolf Kraki was a Skjoldung, a scion of one of the foremost dynasties of ancient Scandinavia. Hundreds of years after this Danish royal house of the Migration Period had passed from the scene, both its origin and its membership remained subjects of intense interest and sharp debate throughout the Scandinavian and Anglo-Saxon worlds. Indeed, the legends about the Skjoldungs were a facet of shared cultural identity throughout the North. According to Sven Aggesen, a Danish monk who wrote late in the twelfth century a Latin history of the Danish kings, the dynasty's founder was called *Skjold* 'Shield' because 'his excellent defence tirelessly protected all the borders of the kingdom'. *Hrolf's Saga* is the principal surviving source of the story regarding this famous dynasty.

Remnants of the Icelandic *Saga of the Skjoldungs* (*Skjöldunga Saga*), an anonymous history of Denmark's ancient kings, also yield much background information about Hrolf's family. From the founder Skjold, the text traces the line through twenty generations. The account ends with Gorm the Old, a Viking Age king who died around the year 940 at the dawn of the historical era in the North. The *Saga of the Skjoldungs* is one of the earliest written sagas of whose existence there is evidence. It may have been already on parchment before 1200, which would mean that it originated in the period just at the start of saga writing in Iceland. We do know that a saga about the Skjoldungs existed in some form in the 1220s, when Snorri Sturluson relied on it as a source for sections of his *Prose Edda*. Unfortunately, the original text was lost in the seventeenth century, but a sixteenth-century Latin summary still exists. Numerous authors and historians from the early thirteenth to the seventeenth century used the saga as a source for their writings which, together with the Latin summary, make it possible to reconstruct a substantial part of the original.

The *Saga of the Skjoldungs* would appear to preserve very old traditions. It asserts, for instance, that the Skjoldung family was of divine origin, descended from 'Scioldus, the son of a certain Odinus, who is called by the common people Othinus'. In a manner acceptable to Christians, the Skjoldung text cloaked this connection with the god by describing Odin as a powerful man who originally came from Asia. In claiming descent from Odin, the *Saga of the Skjoldungs* relies on Norwegian tradition, which differs from information offered by Danish medieval commentators. The differing medieval interpretations of the origin of the family are evidence of embryonic national sentiment. Most of the Danish commentators, including Saxo Grammaticus, traced the family's royal origin from a mythic founder named Dan. The Danish view notwithstanding, the Icelandic/Norwegian version of the story preserved in the *Saga of the Skjoldungs* is certainly older. Snorri Sturluson, who relied on several sources including oral story and verse, corroborates the genealogy. The claim of divine descent from Odin is by no means unique to the Skjoldungs. Such claims were part of a pattern widespread among Germanic dynasties. Other legendary/mythic houses, such as the Volsungs and their descendants, Norway's medieval dynasty, likewise traced their lineage in whole or in part to the father of the gods.

Awareness of the fame of the Skjoldungs' first human founder allows the modern reader to form an idea of the extent of the legendary material that surrounded Hrolf's family in the earlier and later Middle Ages. Writing in Denmark in the twelfth century, Saxo Grammaticus described Skjold as a just and righteous ruler who possessed extraordinary strength. As evidence of his youthful prowess, Saxo reports Skjold's boyhood encounter with a menacing bear:

In his youth, Skjold won fame among his father's huntsmen by defeating a huge beast, an extraordinary feat that foretold the future quality of his courage. He had requested permission from the guardians who were carefully raising him to watch the hunting, when he met a bear of exceptional size. Although Skjold was unarmed, he nevertheless succeeded in tying the bear up with his belt, and then he gave it to his companions to kill.

Skjold also connects *Hrolf's Saga* and *Beowulf*. Skjold is called Scyld Scefing in *Beowulf* and is noted there as a prominent ancestor. *Beowulf* opens with an account of the miraculous origin of the Danish dynasty, telling how Scyld Scefing, while still a child, was from some unspecified place mysteriously set adrift in a small boat. Carried over the sea to Denmark, Scyld Scefing arrived unencumbered by any previous ties. By force of character and strength of arms, Scyld rose to a position of great power.

Although not exactly parallel to the biblical story, the tale of the child from across the water is a widespread motif that at once recalls the story of Moses. Perhaps in part because of this connection, the account of Scyld's mysterious arrival did not die out in Anglo-Saxon times; instead, it continued to arouse interest in England after the Norman conquest. According to William of Malmesbury who in the early twelfth century wrote a *History of the Kings of the English* (*Gesta Regum Anglorum*), the epithet *Scefing*, 'of the sheaf', was given to the boy by the people who found his boat washed up on the shore because 'a handful of grain' accompanied the sleeping child. The founder of the Danish royal dynasty was thus linked with two symbols of successful kingship: the shield, representing the protection of military strength, and the sheaf, suggesting the fertility of the land.

In Iceland, by the period of saga writing, the Skjoldungs' fame had acquired a new venue. Prominent Icelandic families, presuming to be of distant royal descent, now claimed the aura of the family's divine origin. This 'ancestral' connection with the Skjoldungs is a factor that may have contributed to the ongoing interest in the dynasty and especially in Hrolf, its most famous king. The mixture of influences contributing to Icelandic self-identity during the saga-writing era can be seen in the example of the powerful Oddaverjar family from the south of Iceland. Among those identified as family ancestors in a twelfth-century genealogy called *Forefathers' List (Langfeðatal)*, are the biblical Adam, the kings of Troy (including Priam), the god Odin, as well as a number of the Skjoldung kings, among them Halfdan, Helgi, Hroar and Hrolf Kraki. At the very least the Skjoldungs were thought to be worthy of good company.

The Icelandic fascination with the Skjoldungs and in particular with King Hrolf is attested to by still another major Icelandic text. *The Book of Settlements (Landnámabók)*, written principally in the twelfth and thirteenth centuries, gives information about Iceland's first settlers. Among its many entries it tells a curious story about one of Iceland's original settlers, who, around the year 900, entered the by then ancient grave mound of King Hrolf and his warriors. Before coming to Iceland this colonist, named Skeggi of Midfjord, raided as a Viking in the Baltic. While in Denmark, he broke into Hrolf's grave mound, where he found more than just the king's treasure and remains. Skeggi stole Hrolf's sword Skofnung, Hjalti's axe and other valuables. Skeggi, however, went too far when he tried to steal Bodvar's famed sword, Laufi. Bodvar, still on watch after all those centuries, attacked Skeggi, and the situation was perilous for the grave robber until King Hrolf rose to his defence. With that powerful assistance, Skeggi escaped, taking the treasures with him. Did the medieval Icelanders believe such stories? It is hard to say. The concept that the dead live on in their burial mounds is well known in Icelandic lore, usually but not exclusively in descriptions of places distant from Iceland.

Whatever the medieval Icelanders' belief was in stories of the living dead, the sword Skofnung had a history of its own half a millennium after Hrolf's death. In Iceland Skeggi lent Skofnung to the poet Kormak for use in a duel. The sword was returned and later Skeggi's son lent

Skofnung to his kinsman Thorkel, the fourth husband of Gudrun in *Laxdæla Saga*. Their son Gellir took the sword with him on a pilgrimage to Rome. Gellir died on his way home (*c*. 1073) and was buried at Roskilde (Hroar's spring), the town adjacent to Lejre from where the sword was first taken. Knowledge of Skofnung ends at this point.

## Archaeology and the Legendary Hleidargard

According to *Hrolf's Saga*, the seat of the Skjoldung dynasty was Hleidargard. *Gard* means courtyard, farm, estate or stronghold and the Icelandic information about Hleidargard corresponds to information from medieval Denmark. As early as the twelfth century, Danish historians associated the legendary Hleidr with the small village of Lejre on the central Danish island of Sjælland. Lejre, a site with a long history of prehistoric habitation, lies a short distance inland from Roskilde. It is surrounded by Stone Age and Bronze Age mounds and there are many indications of Iron Age habitation.

There is little doubt that in the early Middle Ages Hleidr was a centre of power, and, although there is no sure proof, it has often been surmised that it was the site of Heorot, the Danish hall to which Beowulf came, or a similar royal dwelling. In any event, both *Hrolf's Saga* and *Beowulf* treat the state of the king's hall as an indication of royal strength. In *Beowulf* the fiend Grendel ravages Heorot, whereas in the saga a troll-like dragon comes to Hleidargard, destroying the king's peace.

Following earlier, sometimes romantic investigations, systematic archaeology began at Lejre in the 1940s. Major finds were discovered in 1986–8 when excavations under the leadership of the Danish archaeologist Tom Christensen uncovered traces of a huge (48.3 meters in length by 11.5 meters in width), possibly royal, Viking Age hall. Dated by radiocarbon to the mid-ninth century, the hall stands partially on top of an earlier hall of similar size and construction, from around the year 660 AD. Because of the way the two structures sat, one on top of the other, the decision was made to concentrate on the better preserved and more accessible Viking Age building, diminishing somewhat our knowledge of the older hall. A small number of artifacts that were

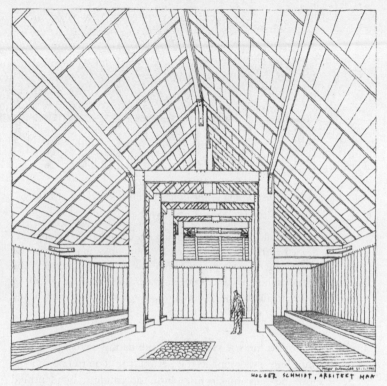

HOLGER SCHMIDT, ARKITEKT MAA

*Illustration 1. Interior of the reconstructed ninth-century Great Hall at Lejre.*

Excavations led by the Danish archaeologist Tom Christensen uncovered the remains of two halls built successively on the same spot. These huge buildings, one from the mid-seventh-century Migration Period, the other from the ninth-century Viking Age, stood at the centre of a settlement. Pictured above is a reconstruction of the interior of the Viking Age hall. On both sides against the walls are tiered side benches where people sat and slept at assigned places. At mealtimes, tables were placed in front of the benches. In the centre of the floor are stones for the fire. The unusually high ceiling allowed smoke to rise and escape through ports at each end of the roof. The steeply pitched roof was supported by two interior rows of massive timbers or 'posts', whose size may be judged by comparison with the man at centre right and the door at the far end.

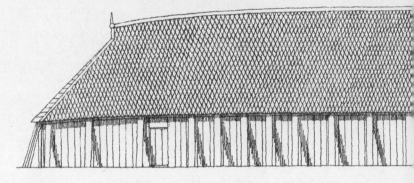

*Illustration 2. Reconstruction of the ninth-century Great Hall at Lejre*
*(43.3 metres in length)*

A massive wooden building, this princely Viking Age dwelling covered approximately 500 sq. metres. The largest hall thus far found in Scandinavia, its size can be judged from the man entering the door toward the middle right. The gables at either end of the curved roof ridge were probably ported to let smoke escape. The end view (Illustration 3) details the shingled roof construction and the covered walkway under the eaves of the roof.

found in and around the site corroborate the dating of the great halls and the surrounding settlement to the period from 600 to 900.

The oldest of the halls appears just a little too young to be identified with Beowulf's Heorot or Hleidargard of *Hrolf's Saga*. It is, however, possible that these halls replaced an older structure in the vicinity, whose remains have been obscured or have yet to be found. The large nearby burial mound called Grydehøj, 'Pot Mound', is evidence of earlier chieftains being connected with the site. Dated by radiocarbon and artifacts, including gold threads and pieces of bronze, to approximately AD 550, the Grydehøj mound was a rich burial. It contained one of the few princely graves known from the Migration Period in Denmark and was most likely erected for a person of considerable political power.

The presence of a ninth-century hall at Lejre may also have been a strong influence on the reinvigoration, in the Viking period, of older legends about the site. Medieval literary accounts preserve the memory of Lejre's social and political prominence during the Viking

HOLGER SCHMIDT, ARKITEKT MAA

*Illustration 3.
End view
(11.5 metres in
width)*

*Illustration 4.
Cross section of the
Viking Age hall*

Much of the archaeological evidence for the hall comes from the remains of the 'post holes'. These were pits that anchored the lower ends of the massive interior vertical timbers and the smaller angled exterior 'raking posts' that supported the ends of the roof and walls. See the subterranean portion of illustration 4.

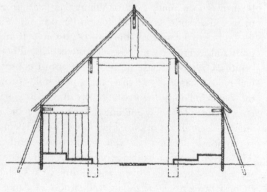

INTRODUCTION

Age. For example, the German chronicler Thietmar of Merseburg knew Lejre as an important capital and pagan cult site. In 1015 he wrote the following description of Lejre based on information learned earlier in 934 when, the German Emperor Henry I had invaded Denmark:

I have heard strange stories about their sacrificial victims in ancient times, and I will not allow the practice to go unmentioned. In one place called Lederun (Lejre), the capital of the realm in the district of Selon (Sjælland), all the people gathered every nine years in January, that is after we have celebrated the birth of the Lord, and there they offered to the gods ninety-nine men and just as many horses, along with dogs and hawks.


## The Saga of King Hrolf Kraki and Beowulf

The Anglo-Saxons were well aware that their own ancestry derived, at least in part, from the Danes. It is therefore not surprising that the

*Illustration 5. Archaeological plan of the two Great Halls at Lejre from the seventh and ninth centuries*

Remains of the ninth-century Viking Age hall, in grey, sit over a less well-preserved seventh-century Migration Period hall, in black. Clearly visible are the outline of the walls and the rows of post holes from both interior supporting posts and exterior raking posts. The two halls, although separated by several centuries, appear to have been of very similar construction. The Viking Age hall reused a row of external raking post holes (marked by an arrow) from the older building. Incorporating existing post holes greatly simplified the construction of the new building and suggests that the later hall was built shortly after the demolition of the earlier one. The archaeology presents a picture of continuous habitation between at least two periods of massive construction. The site shows much evidence of repair over the centuries and some post holes were reused perhaps as many as five times. Cow, sheep and pig bones found in post holes from the oldest hall carbon-14 date to around the year 660. Remnants of bone from the Viking Age building date to *c.* 890. (All illustrations by permission, Tom Christensen, Roskilde Museum)

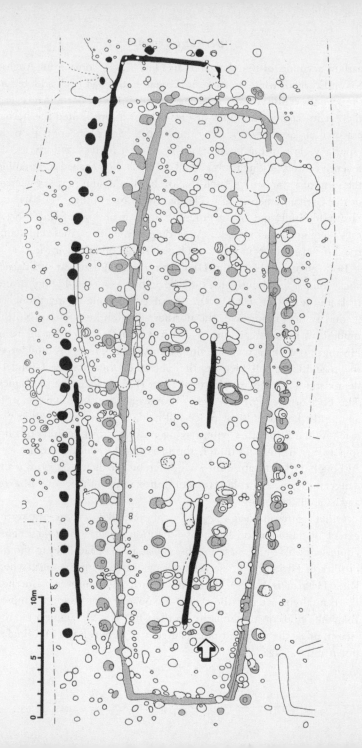

10m

5

0

earliest accounts of the characters in *Hrolf's Saga* come from Anglo-Saxon England, where writing in Roman letters had been adopted in the seventh century, several centuries earlier than in Scandinavia. For the Anglo-Saxons, the kings of Norse legend represented the heroic era of their own history. This trans-North Sea connection is made especially clear in the poem *Widsith*, written perhaps as early as the seventh century, though it may be later. *Widsith* is shaped to resemble the song of a wandering Anglo-Saxon bard, unfolding his knowledge of the Germanic heroic age. The poet tells of Hrothgar (Hroar) and Hrothulf (Hrolf) and, in agreement with the genealogy of *Hrolf's Saga*, calls them uncle and nephew. According to the poem, these chieftains ruled for many years in peace at Heorot, overcoming their foes.

Both **Hro**thulf/Hrolf and **Hro**thgar/Hroar also appear in *Beowulf*, and a comparison shows some differences between the Old English and Icelandic stories. In *Hrolf's Saga* Hroar is a notable figure, though a secondary one, ruling over the northern English kingdom of Northumberland until forced into a disastrous conflict. In *Beowulf*, King Hrothgar is a character of central importance. He is the builder of the magnificent hall Heorot, the object of the monster Grendel's depredations. Moreover, Hrothgar, as in *Widsith*, is king of the Danes. The poet of *Beowulf* hints darkly, however, that there will be strife among the kinsmen: 'their peace still held, each one to the other was true'. When Hrothgar's wife, having no real choice, commends her sons to her nephew Hrothulf, she fears that he will do them harm. Although the stories are somewhat different, the theme of betrayal and danger in the uncle–nephew relationship exists in both the Anglo-Saxon and Scandinavian stories.

Other figures in *Hrolf's Saga* also appear in *Beowulf*, attesting to the extent of the common legendary tradition. Halga (the Old English equivalent of Helgi) is noted in *Beowulf* as a son of Healfdeane and the brother of Hrothgar. These relationships agree with the saga, where King Halfdan is Helgi's father and Hroar is his brother. But it is the central character of the Anglo-Saxon text, the young champion Beowulf, who, in his similarity to the Old Norse champion Bodvar Bjarki, offers the most intriguing agreement between the Old English poem and the saga.

## Beowulf and Bodvar Bjarki: The Bear Warriors

Scholars have long noted similarities between the stories of Bodvar Bjarki and Beowulf. The parallels, ranging from shared details to broad plot-resemblances, are significant enough to warrant the supposition that the two stories are somehow related. For example, the stories of both heroes begin in the land of the Gotar (Old Norse *Gautar*, Old English *Geatas*) where each hero is related to the king. Both heroes have names that approximate to the word 'bear': Bjarki means 'little bear', and Beowulf is a compound that may mean 'bee-wolf', a plausible description for 'bear', the animal that shares with man a liking for honey. Less likely is the possibility that the name is formed from the words *beorn* 'bear' and *ulf* 'wolf'. Each hero journeys across water to come to the Danish court, ruled by a member of the Skjoldung dynasty. In each instance the warrior who comes from outside the society acts as a 'land cleanser', removing a non-human threat to the king's authority. In both stories the Danish court is being threatened by a monster who conducts raids in the night and against whom the king's retainers are helpless. Reflective, perhaps, of the many centuries separating the writing of the Old English and the Icelandic texts, the monsters are described differently. In the fourteenth-century saga the attacking creature is called a 'great troll', but is described as a winged dragon breathing fire, a later type of medieval monster. The Anglo-Saxon epic contains a more chthonic creature, a human-hating monster who lives underground in the dangerous marshy outlands.

Such similarities suggest that *Beowulf* preserves strands of some of the legends that eventually coalesced to form *Hrolf's Saga*. But what was this narrative legacy? The answer is found in part in Bodvar's overt connection with the bear, an animal with many human characteristics. Bears can walk upright on two feet and have eyes similar to those of humans, giving the impression of intelligence and a capacity for human emotions. The connection between bear and man, which is an old one, is intensified by the fact that the two traditionally live on the borders of each other's realms and share part of each other's space. Man, who claims the agricultural fields and grazing meadows, makes hunting and gathering incursions into the forest. The bear, who lives in the wild of the forest, makes incursions into the world of men, especially into areas where livestock are kept. If the forest line, the boundary between nature on the one hand and culture on the other, separates the home regions of bear and man, it does not limit the activity of either. The bear, supreme in his world, and man, the master of his, frequently meet. The resultant unavoidable contest, almost between equals, traditionally has bred a relationship of respect and fear. On the part of men, at least, there is a long tradition of psychological curiosity and confused identity. From this uneasy relationship arose an ancient and varied narrative legacy.

Preserved in an Icelandic saga, the story of Bodvar Bjarki may represent one version of a folktale type distributed throughout Europe, Asia, Africa and America. In the late nineteenth century, the German scholar Friedrich Panzer called this folktale type the Bear's Son Tale. Today it is more commonly identified as the Three Stolen Princesses, after a motif present in some versions but not in the story of Bjarki. The hero of this type of tale is frequently the offspring of a human woman and a bear. He is exceedingly strong and he may have some bearlike traits. In some versions, as in the saga, he wins a weapon of extraordinary power as an heirloom from his father. As he travels throughout the world, he acquires companions who possess remarkable strength and helpful capabilities. Together, the hero and his companions come to an empty house. Its owner, a monster of some sort, returns home and mistreats one of the hero's companions. The hero wounds the monster, follows it to the underworld and kills it.

It is clear that Bjarki's origins and childhood resemble the Bear's Son Tale. Bjarki's brothers, or his comrade Hjalti, may also be seen as the companions from the folktale, although they can likewise be interpreted in the light of epic companionship. If Bjarki's story displays traditional folktale elements, his character as developed in the saga has larger epic proportions than those normally attributed to a folktale hero. This larger dimension is seen in Bjarki's later adventures, which less closely parallel the folktale type. Nevertheless, the distinction between epic and folktale hero is often unclear, and it is likely that Bodvar's heroic character has roots in the two related forms of oral narration. The monster who raids

Hrolf's hall may be identified in several ways: on the one hand, as the demonic owner of the house; and, on the other, as one of the epic forces of chaos. *Beowulf* likewise has been interpreted as a version of the Bear's Son Tale. Although Beowulf's youth lacks the Bear's Son motifs, his battle with Grendel follows the tale-type much more closely than does Bjarki's dragon-slaying exploit. Since the stories of Beowulf and Bodvar share so many similarities, in both overt detail and underlying structure, it is possible that the origin of their affinities lies in an older Scandinavian version of the Bear's Son Tale.

Whatever the ultimate origin of Bjarki's story, a number of additional factors connect him with the bear. Indeed, Bodvar Bjarki, the offspring of a bear, is primarily distinctive because of his intimate connection with the animal. The names of Bodvar's parents, Bjorn and Bera, mean 'bear' and 'she-bear', and 'Bjarki' means 'bear-cub' or 'little bear'. It is quite possible that Bjarki was his original name and Bodvar, derived from the Old Norse word *böð* meaning 'battle', is a nickname carrying the meaning 'warlike'. If so, the hero's full name means something like 'Fierce-'/'Battle-Bjarki(-Bear)'.

One thing that is certain is that the saga's eerie story of Bodvar's mother coupling with a doomed bear is ancient. The story of the woman who has offspring by a bear is rooted in the storytelling and the ceremonial practices of bear hunters throughout the northern hemisphere. In such societies the hunted bear is usually treated as a human or a superhuman being. Just as Bjorn in the saga, the bear is assumed to foresee its own death and is often thought of as voluntarily surrendering to the hunters. In Lapland, a brass ring sometimes played a role in the ceremonies of bear hunters; and in the saga Bjorn is loved by a magical Lappish princess and then identified by a ring hidden in his flesh. Further, in keeping with the story presented in the saga, Scandinavian bear stories sometimes reveal a sexual connection between the hunted bear and a human woman. Sometimes great families among bear hunters trace their lineage to a marriage between a human and a bear.

Remnants of the Scandinavian tradition of the bear found in the saga survived well into modern times in the Trondelag region of northern Norway. In the 1920s and 1930s Anton Röstad, a resident from the inland district of Verdal, collected local folktales and legends with the assistance of Professor Nils Lid and published them in a volume called *Frå gamal tid* (From the Past). Several of the tales of this region, which borders on the forest, display elements of *Hrolf's Saga*, among them the story of Bjorn and his love for Bera, an episode that the saga places in Norway. One tale describes how a woman named Beret, afterward called Bjorn-Beret ('Bear-Beret'), was carried off by a bear:

One time there was a young woman, who was called Bjorn-Beret. She was taken by the bear. He took her with him into his lair and there she lived for a long time together with the bear. She had a child with the bear and he treated her well. Each day, a bowl of milk was passed in to her. But one day the bowl was full of blood. The bear had been shot and so she went back to the inhabited areas.

Another tale collected by Röstad, omitting the story of the bear's sad demise, presents the woman and her ursine consort as the progenitors of a local family:

There was a girl from Vuku who was taken by the bear and lived for a time with him in the lair. She also had a child with the bear, and it is said that there is still a family descended from them.

The folk memory of Verdal also included notions of men transformed into bears and the association of such bears with women. The following story is of especial interest because Bodvar's father was changed into a bear by a spell:

The bear never touched pregnant women. Some bears liked to follow such women but by no means all bears did that. Those who were inclined to follow the women were men who had been transformed into bears.

However one interprets the Bear's Son material, the Bear's Son motif exists in legend and myth as well as folktale. It is this type of folkloristic material that inspires saga and epic and comes from a deep wellspring of cultural tradition.

# Berserkers

Berserkers, so prominent in *Hrolf's Saga*, are the remnants in Christian times of older stories. In pre-Christian Scandinavia berserkers seem to have been members of cults connected with Odin in his capacity as god of warriors. Snorri Sturluson in *Ynglinga Saga*, recalling numerous elements of ancient lore, describes Odin's warriors in this way:

His men went to battle without armour and acted like mad dogs or wolves. They bit into their shields and were as strong as bears or bulls. They killed men, but neither fire nor iron harmed them. This madness is called berserker-fury.

The berserkers of the saga, who often appear as the core of the king's warband, are at times reminiscent of the retinue of warriors surrounding Odin and may ultimately derive from ancient bear cults. Debate has centred on the meaning of the word itself. *Berserker* could mean 'bare shirt', that is, naked; berserkers, as a mark of ferocity and invincibility, are said to have fought without needing armour. The word, however, may also mean 'bear-shirt', reflective of the shape and nature of the bear assumed by these warriors. More literally, it may refer to protective bearskins that such warriors may have worn into battle. When the 'berserker rage' was upon him, a berserker was thought of as a sort of 'were-bear' (or werewolf), part man, part beast, who was neither fully human nor fully animal. Although not specifically so called, Bodvar Bjarki is a berserker of sorts. He appears at Hrolf's final battle in the form of a huge bear, invulnerable to weapons. In both his invulnerability and his ability to change shape, Bodvar also displays preternatural abilities resembling those of Odinic champions.

# Myth in the Saga

*Hrolf's Saga* contains many traces of the mythology of Odin. In Eddic poetry Odin is called both *Sigtýr*, 'god of victory', and *Sigfaðir*, 'father of victory'. It is in this capacity – as the giver of victory – that Odin appears in the saga. That is the role which Odin plays in Hrolf's struggle with the miserly King Adils of Sweden. Calling himself Hrani, the god repeatedly tests Hrolf's men, as if Odin is determining in advance which ones will be able to withstand the ordeals awaiting them at Adils' court. The warriors who fail are successively sent home so that in the end only Hrolf's finest champions accompany their chieftain into the hostile court of Adils. Not surprisingly, the heroes chosen by Odin have characteristics similar to those displayed by the god himself. For instance, Svipdag, one of the more mysterious characters in the saga, resembles Odin in that he controls the destiny of a certain group of warriors. Svipdag is also one-eyed, like Odin, who in Norse myth sacrificed an eye for a drink of wisdom from Mimir's well at the foot of the world tree.

Odin is also a fickle god, whose complex and vengeful nature plays a crucial role in *Hrolf's Saga*. Bjarki curses Odin for his treachery, but the god is simply acting in character. Odin's propensity to betray even his most beloved heroes, especially those to whom he had previously granted a long string of victories, is well known. Saxo Grammaticus's telling of the tale of another early Danish king, Harald Wartooth, helps to explain both the motivation attributed to Odin and Hrolf's acceptance of the god's actions. One day Harald Wartooth went into battle only to find his opponent using the wedge formation, a battle tactic that was Odin's special gift to Harald. Aware of the danger of gods and shape shifters, the king suddenly looked at his charioteer Bruni, realizing that here was his old friend Odin. Harald entreated the god, reminding Odin of his earlier kindly acts toward the Danes. The king asked the god to grant him this final victory. In return, Harald promised to dedicate to Odin the souls of those slain in the fighting. Unmoved by the king's prayers, Bruni suddenly knocked Harald from his chariot, grabbed the king's mace and struck Harald his deathblow. Thus Odin killed Harald Wartooth with the king's own weapon.

Although the author of *Hrolf's Saga* seems to delight in chronicling the dark nature of the pagan god, it does not follow that the accusation that Odin is guilty of treachery is only a mark of Christian influence. Odin's actions in the saga make sense in the context of pre-Christian myth. The god collects dead heroes because he needs them to fight on his side at Ragnarok, the great battle at the end of time when monsters will destroy the world and the demonic Fenris Wolf will kill Odin himself. Scenes from another heroic text, *Eiriksmál*, a lay memorializing a tenth-century Norwegian Eirik Bloodaxe, king of Norway for a time and then the Viking king of York, help to explain the Norse cultural understanding of both Odin's motivation and Hrolf's fate. When Odin is challenged in the poem to explain why he has denied victory to so splendid a warrior as Eirik, the god of war replies: 'Because a grey wolf glares at the dwellings of the gods.'

The saga author seems to have had uneasy feelings concerning Odin as the arbitrator of victory. In the view of fourteenth-century Scandinavians, the Christian God was the only true god of victory. This Christian perspective is apparent when the saga writer uncharacteristically moralizes: 'Human strength cannot withstand such fiendish power, unless the strength of God is employed against it. That alone stood between you and victory, King Hrolf . . . you had no knowledge of your Creator.'

## Christian Influence

Even though *Hrolf's Saga*, like other Icelandic mythic–heroic texts, preserves remnants of the cult of Odin, it is, as noted above, infused with Christian values. Uneasy at times, this mixture is not surprising, for the saga was written three or four centuries after Iceland's conversion to Christianity in 1000. When, for instance, King Adils of Sweden is condemned as an idolater and a practitioner of magic, the author's convictions become clear: Adils was not simply bad; he was evil in all ways possible. Whatever the saga author's convictions, Adils appears to have been a historical king of the Swedes, one who was known for his attachment to pagan belief. Snorri Sturluson recounts in *The Saga of the Ynglings* that Adils died from a horse fall while taking part in a pagan sacrifice-ritual.

But the saga author may have had conflicting emotions toward his subject matter. There is no doubt that the writer was aware that the material came from the pre-Christian past, and it may be that a penchant for old stories, especially stories intimately connected with Odin, was potentially controversial. Almost as an afterthought, perhaps out of conscience or to protect himself from accusation, the saga writer attempts to separate Hrolf and the king's champions from too close a pagan connection by writing: 'It is not mentioned that King Hrolf and his champions at any time worshipped the old gods. Rather, they put their trust in their own might and main. The holy faith, at that time, had not been proclaimed here in the northern lands and, for this reason, they who lived in the North had little knowledge of their Creator.'

## Conclusion

*The Saga of King Hrolf Kraki* is both a treasure of fourteenth-century Icelandic prose writing and a significant repository of often ancient legend, epic, myth, cultic memory and folktale. At almost the very last moment in the Middle Ages when the earlier ideas about King Hrolf, his ancestors and his champions still formed a vigorous and active part of living memory, a saga writer turned his attention to the material. As a result the memory of an important chapter in the oldest ages of Scandinavia's past was preserved. Around the year 1200 Saxo wrote, 'The diligence of the men of Iceland must not be shrouded in silence.' His words are as true today as they were then, when he turned for inspiration to many of the same Icelandic stories included in *Hrolf's Saga*.

# Map: The World of
## *The Saga of King Hrolf Kraki*

Centred in Denmark, the action of the saga spreads over most of Scandinavia and a large area of Northern Europe. This map names some of the major lands and seas while locating the following sites and kingdoms:

ENGLAND: King Nordri, father of Ogn the wife of Hroar, ruled over part of England.

DENMARK: Kingdom of Hrolf, ruled from his stronghold at Hleidargard. Early in the saga, Halfdan rules Denmark until deposed by his jealous brother Frodi. Halfdan's son Helgi recovers the kingship and rules until slain. He is succeeded by his son Hrolf.

FINNMARK: The home of Hvit in far northern Scandinavia.

FYRIS PLAINS: Plains in Sweden, located south of Uppsala. Hrolf scatters gold on the Fyris Plains, distracting the pursuing forces of King Adils.

GAUTLAND: The kingdom of Bodvar Bjarki's brother, Thorir Hound's Foot. Located in southwestern Sweden.

HLEIDARGARD: King Hrolf's royal seat, located on the central island of Sjælland. Today, the modern town of Lejre near Roskilde (Hroar's Spring).

NORTHUMBERLAND: The kingdom of Hroar, Halfdan's son, located in northeastern England.

SAXLAND: The kingdom of Queen Olof, mother of Yrsa and grand-mother of Hrolf, located in northern Germany.

SWEDEN: The kingdom ruled by Adils, and the home of farmer Svip, whose son, Svipdag, becomes one of Hrolf's champions.

UPPSALA: Royal seat of Sweden, site of King Adils' court.

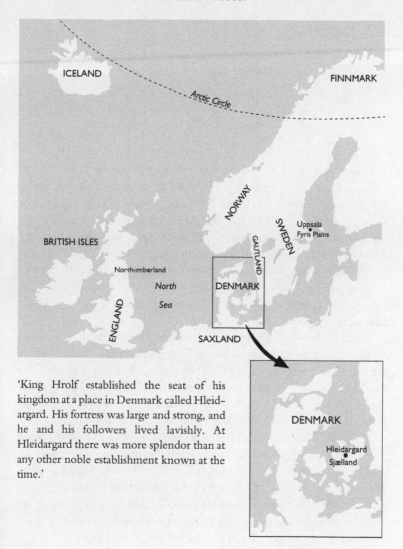

'King Hrolf established the seat of his kingdom at a place in Denmark called Hleidargard. His fortress was large and strong, and he and his followers lived lavishly. At Hleidargard there was more splendor than at any other noble establishment known at the time.'

# Note on the Translation

*The Saga of King Hrolf Kraki* survives in part or whole in over forty paper manuscripts. The earliest of these date from the first part of the seventeenth century and the extant manuscripts almost certainly stem from a single lost original. This translation is based on Desmond Slay's careful edition of the manuscript AM 285 4to, as published in the *Editiones Arnamagnæanæ* series (Copenhagen, 1960). Today the manuscript, which was written in January 1654 by the scribe Brynjólfur Jónsson, contains only *Hrólfs saga kraka*. Originally, however, this text was part of a larger codex, probably written for the Bishops of Hólar in northern Iceland.

I thank Örnólfur Thorsson for sharing his unpublished modern Icelandic adaptation of Slay's edition. So too I thank my former student Jeffrey Mazo for his assistance with the notes. My friend Finnur Torfi Stefánsson spent several winter nights on his farm at Tungufell in Borgarfjörður reading a draft of my translation and I thank him for his suggestions and for his hospitality. Hallfreður Örn Eiríksson, at the Árni Magnússon Manuscript Institute in Reykjavík, helped me work through some of the knottier points of translation and Professors Robert Kellogg and David Dumville offered insightful comments on the Introduction. I also thank my old friends from early days in Iceland, Robert Guillemette, who is still in Reykjavik, and Dominic X. Cooper, now living on Ardnamurchan in Argyll, for their hospitality and discussions while I was translating this saga. Robert designed the illustrations.

The spelling of proper names and special terms in the text has been anglicized, usually by omitting the Old Norse inflectional endings and replacing non-English letters with their closest equivalents. I do not strive for complete consistency, especially when a name is familiar to

English speakers in another form; thus, I use *Valhalla* rather than *Valhöll*. I added chapter titles to aid the reader. My goal throughout has been to produce an accurate, readable translation of an important medieval text.

At the end of the book is a Glossary of Proper Names. I compiled this index to provide the reader with a tool for locating the characters (both human and supernatural), groups, places, animals and objects that appear in the saga. Also at the rear of the volume the reader will find genealogies, notes and a listing of prominent characters in the saga and their equivalents in three other medieval texts.

# THE SAGA OF KING HROLF KRAKI

Here begins the Saga of King Hrolf Kraki,
and first is written the tale of King Frodi

## 1. *King Frodi Kills His Brother King Halfdan*

A man was named Halfdan and another Frodi; the two were brothers.
They were the sons of a king and each ruled his own kingdom.
King Halfdan[1] was mild-mannered and easygoing; he was quiet and
good-natured, but King Frodi was the harshest and greediest of men.
King Halfdan had three children: two of them were sons. The third, a
daughter named Signy, was the eldest.[2] She was married to Jarl Saevil.*
At the time of these events Halfdan's sons were young; one was named
Hroar and the other Helgi.[3] Their foster-father[4] was named Regin, and
he loved the boys deeply.

An island lay a short distance from Halfdan's stronghold; on it lived
a karl or freeman[5] named Vifil.[6] The place, called Vifil's island, was
named for the freeman, who was a lifelong friend of King Halfdan. He
had two hounds, one called Hopp and the other Ho. Vifil was a man
of substance and, if threatened, was well versed in the arts of old magic.

Now it is told that King Frodi stayed home in his kingdom. He
bitterly envied his brother, King Halfdan, because Halfdan alone ruled
Denmark. As King Frodi felt that he had not fared as well, he assembled
a large following of armed men and set out for Denmark.

Arriving in the dead of night, Frodi burned and destroyed everything.
King Halfdan, unable to defend himself, was seized and killed, but some
of his followers managed to escape. All the inhabitants of the stronghold
were forced to swear allegiance to King Frodi; those who refused were
subjected to torture.

Helgi and Hroar's foster father, Regin, helped the boys escape to

---

* 'Jarl' was a noble title, denoting a powerful chieftain, who often ruled his own lands.
The word is related to English 'earl'.

Vifil on his island. They mourned their loss deeply, and Regin said that, if Vifil were unable to hide the boys from King Frodi, 'then all places of shelter will be filled with snow'.* Vifil responded that 'here is a dangerous contest with a powerful adversary,' but he added that it was his obligation to help the boys. He then accepted the boys and led them to an underground room,[7] where they often stayed. During the day they were able to breathe freely in the freeman's woods, because the island was half-covered with forest. The boys were now separated from Regin, who had many valuable estates as well as a wife and children in Denmark. For himself, Regin saw no other way than to submit to King Frodi, swearing to him oaths of allegiance. King Frodi took control of the Danish kingdom, levying tribute and taxes. Most people submitted unwillingly because he was a much despised man. Frodi also laid tribute on Jarl Saevil.

Despite his successes, Frodi did not have peace of mind, because he could nowhere find Helgi or Hroar. He sent his spies everywhere, near and far, north and south, east and west. He promised generous gifts to those who could give him information about the boys. For those who concealed them, he swore tortures upon discovery. Yet no one seemed to know anything to tell the king about the boys.

Then Frodi sought the aid of seeresses and soothsayers[8] in all parts of the land. He had them search the country up and down, even the islands and the outlying rocks. They found nothing.

Now the king sought out sorcerers,[9] who could pry into anything they wished. They told him the boys were not being brought up on land, yet they were not far off from the king, who responded, 'We have searched widely for them, and it seems to me least likely that they are nearby. Nevertheless, there is an island that we have not scoured thoroughly. Almost no one lives on it except for one poor freeman.'

'Search there first,' said the sorcerers, 'because mist and secrecy shroud that island. Only with difficulty can we see the area around this man's house. He seems to be a person of profound learning, and there is more to him than meets the eye.'

---

* A common expression in medieval Iceland, meaning that there would be no chance of finding refuge.

The king replied, 'Then we will search there again, although it seems strange to me that a poor fisherman would harbour the boys, daring to withhold them from me.'

## 2. The Search

Early one morning, Vifil awoke with a sense of foreboding. He said, 'The air and the paths are alive with magic, and powerful spirits[10] have visited the island. Get up, Hroar and Helgi, sons of Halfdan. Keep yourselves hidden today in the underbrush of my woods.'

The boys ran into the woods and events unfolded as the freeman had predicted. King Frodi's messengers arrived on the island and searched for the boys. They looked everywhere they could imagine, but nowhere could they find the brothers. Although the freeman seemed to be of questionable nature, Frodi's men left. They had accomplished nothing and reported to the king that they were unable to find the boys.

'You have searched poorly,' said the king. 'That man is skilled in magic. Now retrace your steps and then return there immediately so that the freeman will not have time to hide them again, if they are there.'

The men, obliged to do as the king commanded, went once again to the island. Vifil said to the boys, 'This is not the time to be sitting around inside. Head for the woods as quickly as you can.' They did so, arriving before the king's men rushed in, demanding the right to search.

Vifil had everything opened up for the searchers. But, wherever they looked, the king's men could not find the boys on the island. They then returned and reported the lack of success to the king.

King Frodi answered, 'We will no longer deal leniently with this man. Tomorrow I myself will go to the island.' And the result was that the king himself did go.

Vifil awoke troubled. He quickly realized that he had to devise a plan. He told the brothers to be 'aware that, if I call loudly to my dogs, Hopp and Ho, you must run to your underground shelter. Calling to the dogs is a signal that danger has come on to the island. You will

3

need to protect yourselves, for now your kinsman Frodi himself is in the hunt. He seeks your lives with all kinds of schemes and tricks, and it is no longer clear that I will be able to keep you safe.'

Then Vifil went down to the shore. The king's ship had already landed, but Vifil acted as if he saw nothing, walking around as though looking for his sheep. He carried on in this way, concentrating so hard that he never once looked toward the king or his men. The king ordered his men to seize Vifil. They did so and then led him to the king.

'You are a crafty sort,' said the king, 'and a cunning one too. Now tell me where the princes are, because you must surely know.'

The freeman replied, 'Greetings, my lord, but do not hold me, for if you do the wolf will tear my sheep apart.' He then called loudly, 'Hopp and Ho, look after the sheep, because I cannot save them.'

The king said, 'What are you shouting now?'

The man replied, 'My dogs are named in that way. Search as freely as you desire, Sire. I do not suppose that the princes will be found here, and I am amazed that you think that I would hide anyone from you.'

The king said, 'You are without doubt a sly one. But this time the boys will not be able to conceal themselves, although they have succeeded thus far. It would be fitting if I were to take your life.'

'That is now within your power,' replied the freeman. 'Should you so decide, then you will have accomplished something on the island, rather than leaving with matters as they now stand.'

The king said, 'I cannot be bothered to kill you, although it seems to me that not doing so is ill-advised.' Then he sailed home. Vifil now went to tell the boys that they could no longer stay there: 'I will send you to Jarl Saevil, your brother-in-law. You will become famous men if you live long enough.'

## 3. *The Boys Helgi and Hroar Revealed*

Hroar was then twelve years old, but Helgi who was only ten was the bigger and more courageous of the two. The boys now left the island. They called themselves Ham and Hrani wherever they went or when-

4

ever they spoke with people.[11] The boys reached Jarl Saevil's estate, but then let a week pass before they asked the jarl for permission to stay. The jarl replied, 'From you two I think I will acquire little, but I will not deny you food, at least for awhile.' The brothers stayed there for a time but proved to be troublesome. Neither their rank nor their family was known. Even the jarl did not suspect who they were, since they had told him nothing about themselves.

Some men, saying that the boys were born with scurvy on their heads, mocked them as they always wore hooded cloaks. Because the boys never pushed back their hoods, many thought their heads were covered with sores and vermin. The brothers stayed there into the third winter.

Next it happened that King Frodi invited Jarl Saevil to a feast. The king's suspicions were aroused that Saevil might be hiding the boys because of their kinship. The jarl prepared for the journey, intending to take a large following. The boys volunteered to go, but the jarl refused. Signy, the jarl's wife, went along on the journey.

Ham, who was really Helgi in disguise, found for himself an unbroken colt to ride. Once seated on it, he raced after the company, riding backward, thus facing the tail. He behaved in every way like a fool. His brother, Hrani, finding a similar mount, rode facing the correct way.

The jarl now saw that the boys were following him and that they were unable to manage their horses. The shaggy colts leapt backwards and forwards under them, and Hrani's hood fell down. Signy, their sister, noticed and immediately recognized them. She began to sob deeply. The jarl asked her why she was crying. Signy spoke this verse:

1. All the royal family
   of the Skjoldungs'
   princely grove
   have become limbs only.[12]
   My brothers, riding
   bareback, I saw,
   but Saevil's men sit on
   saddled horses.

'This is good news,' said the jarl, 'but keep it from becoming known.'

He then rode back to the boys, asking them to go home. He called them a disgrace to a company of good men. By then both boys were walking, and the jarl spoke in this way so as not to expose them. But the boys, refusing to turn back, moved to the fringes of the escort and travelled at the far rear of the company.

When they arrived at the feast, Helgi and Hroar ran back and forth in the hall. At one point, this activity brought them to the place where Signy, their sister, was sitting. She whispered to them, 'Do not stay in the hall, because you are not yet fully grown.' But they paid no attention to her warning.

King Frodi then started to speak. He announced that he wanted the sons of King Halfdan found and promised, for his part, to show great honour to the man who could tell him something about the boys.

Then a seeress who was called Heid arrived.[13] The king told her to use her art to divine what she could learn about the boys. The king had a magnificent feast prepared for her and had her placed on a high trance platform.[14] Then he asked what she could see of the future, 'because I know,' he said, 'that much will be made clear to you. I see that there is great luck in you, so answer me as quickly as possible.'

She wrenched open her jaws and yawned deeply, and this chant emerged from her mouth:

2. Two are the men
   I trust in neither,
   they the excellent ones
   who sit by the fire's side.

The king replied, 'Are you speaking about the boys or about those who have saved them?' She answered,

3. They who long were
   on Vifil's island
   and there were hailed
   with hounds' names,
   Hopp and Ho.

Just then Signy threw a gold ring to the Sybil. Heid was pleased with the gift, and she wanted to stop her divining. She said, 'This is how matters stand. What I said is only a lie, and now all my prophecies have gone astray.'

The king replied, 'If you do not choose more wisely, you will be tortured into speaking. Here among so many people, I still do not understand any better than previously what you are saying. And why is Signy not in her seat? Can it be that wolves are plotting with predators?'[15]

The king was told that Signy had been sickened by the smoke from the hearth. Jarl Saevil asked her to sit up and behave courageously, 'for it can have much bearing on keeping the boys alive, if that is what is meant to be. Act in such a way that your thoughts cannot be read. As matters stand, there is nothing that we can do to help them.'

King Frodi now pressed the sorceress hard. He commanded her to tell the truth if she did not want to be tortured. Her mouth gaped wide, but the spell became difficult. Finally she spoke this verse:

4. I see where they sit,
    sons of Halfdan,
    Hroar and Helgi,
    healthy both.
    They will rob
    Frodi of life.

'Unless they are quickly dealt with,' she said, 'but that will not happen.'
Then she jumped down from the trance platform and said:

5. Hard are the eyes
    of Ham and Hrani;
    they are princes
    wonderfully bold.

The boys, now frightened, ran from the hall and headed for the woods. Regin, their foster father, recognized them and was much moved. The sorceress, who herself now ran from the hall, had given the boys good advice when she told them to save themselves.

The king ordered his men to rise and chase after the boys. Regin then extinguished all the lights in the hall. Men began to grapple with one another, and some of them held the king's men back. There were those in the hall who wanted to see the boys escape and, because of that intervention, the two reached the woods. King Frodi said, 'They came close this time, and many here have been plotting with them. When I have the time, I will take a fearful vengeance for their doing so. Now, however, we are free to drink all night long. The princes will be so relieved at having escaped that they will first try to save their lives.'

Regin began to serve the ale. In this task he was joined by many of his friends, and they plied the drinks so generously that men passed out and fell, one on top of the other. Meanwhile, the brothers, as noted earlier, hid in the woods.

When the boys had been there awhile, they saw a man riding toward them from the hall. They soon recognized that it was Regin, their foster father. They were pleased to see him and greeted him well, but Regin ignored their greeting. Instead he turned his horse around, facing back toward the hall. The boys wondered at this, asking themselves what this action might mean. Regin turned his horse toward them for a second time, acting now so menacingly that he seemed likely to attack them at any moment. Helgi said, 'I think I know what he wants.'

Regin now rode back to the hall and the boys followed him. 'My foster father behaves in this way,' said Helgi, 'because he does not want to violate his oaths to King Frodi. For this reason he will not speak to us, yet he will gladly help us.'

Near the hall stood a grove of trees owned by the king. When they reached it, Regin said to himself, 'If I sought vengeance against King Frodi for great wrongs, I would burn down this grove.' He said nothing else.

Hroar said, 'What does that mean?'

'He wants us to go back to the hall,' answered Helgi, 'and set it afire, excepting one doorway that leads outside.'

'What can we do?' asked Hroar. 'We are just two boys facing overwhelming odds.'

'Still,' said Helgi, 'we will do it, because we will have to risk it sometime if we are to avenge our losses.' And so they carried out the plan.

The next to tell is Jarl Saevil's emergence from the hall with all his men. He said, 'Let's build up the fire and help these boys. I owe no obligation to King Frodi.'

King Frodi had two smiths who were master craftsmen. Both were named Var. Regin led his own men out through the door of the hall; he also saved his friends and his in-laws.


## 4. The Death of King Frodi

King Frodi now awakened in the hall. Sighing loudly, he said, 'I dreamed a dream, lads. It is one that promises no fair wind, and I will relate it to you. I dreamed that I thought someone was calling to us, saying, "Now you have come home, King, you and your men." I answered, it seemed, angrily, "Home to where?" Then the voice called out again, this time so near to me that I felt the breath of the one calling. "Home to Hel. Home to Hel,"* said the one who called. Then, I awoke.'

Just then, they heard Regin speaking a verse outside the door to the hall:

6. Rain is without,†
   and the warriors of Halfdan,
   tough adversaries,
   say this to Frodi.
   Var the careful forged nails,

---

* *Hel* was the name both for the land of the dead and for the Scandinavian goddess of death and of the underworld.

† *Regin* is the word for 'rain' as well as a man's name. Thus both Regin and rain are outside. The poem is full of double meanings. The smiths' names are Var, meaning 'to be cautious' or 'the careful one'. In the poem's final line, Var makes the *varnagli*, the nail of caution. Because *regin* is also a plural word for the gods, there is a further implication that the gods are involved.

and Var, the wary, formed the heads,
but the smiths worked
warnings for the wary.

Then the king's men, those who were inside, said that it was little news if it was raining outside or if the king's smiths were forging nails or doing other smithy work.

The king said, 'You do not find news in that? It strikes me otherwise, for Regin has told us of some impending danger. He has given a sign of warning and will be sly and cunning with me.'

Next the king, going to the door of the hall, saw that the enemy was in front. By then the whole hall was covered with flames. The king asked who was responsible for the fire. He was told that Helgi was in charge and that his brother Hroar was with him.

The king proposed a truce to the boys. He offered that they alone could set the terms, saying, 'It goes against nature's order that among us kinsmen each man should want to be the killer of the other.'

Helgi replied, 'No one can trust you. You will betray us no less than you betrayed my father Halfdan. Now you must pay for your actions.'

Then the king, turning back from the hall door, went to the entrance of his underground passageway, intending to save himself by escaping into the woods. But when he entered the passageway, he found Regin standing there. As Regin's intentions were not peaceful, the king returned to the hall, where he and most of his followers burned to death. Sigrid, the mother of the brothers Helgi and Hroar, also burned to death inside the hall, because she chose not to leave.

For their support the brothers thanked Jarl Saevil, their brother-in-law; Regin, their foster father; and all the company. To many they gave rich gifts. They took the kingdom, including all of King Frodi's wealth, his lands and his movable property.

The brothers were unlike in temperament. Hroar was mild and easy-going, whereas Helgi was a staunch warrior and was regarded as by far the more important of the two. Matters continued this way for a while.

Here ends the tale of Frodi and now begins the story of Hroar and Helgi, the sons of Halfdan.

KING HELGI ATTEMPTS TO MARRY QUEEN OLOF

## 5. *King Helgi Rules Denmark and King Hroar Marries*

There was a king named Nordri; he ruled over parts of England. His daughter was named Ogn. Hroar spent many years with King Nordri and commanded the defence of the realm. Hroar was a trusted supporter of the king and a deep friendship grew between the two men. After a time Hroar married Ogn[16] and settled there in the kingdom with King Nordri, his father-in-law. Helgi ruled over Denmark, controlling the inheritance from their father.

Jarl Saevil and Signy ruled their own lands.[17] Their son was named Hrok. In Denmark, King Helgi, the son of Halfdan, was unmarried. Regin now took sick and died; it was regarded as a great loss because he was a much loved man.

## 6. *King Helgi Attempts to Marry Queen Olof*

At that time a queen named Olof[18] ruled over Saxland.\* Like a warrior king, she dressed in a coat of mail, carried sword and shield, and wore a helmet. This was her nature: beautiful in looks, yet cruel and arrogant in temperament. Those who knew about such matters said that Olof was the best match in all the northern countries, but she had no intention of marrying any man.

King Helgi heard about this proud queen. It seemed to him that marrying the woman, whether she was willing or not, would increase his fame and importance. So one day he set off with a large company of armed men and, without warning, he landed in the country ruled by the powerful Queen Olof. Helgi sent messengers to her hall, requesting that the queen be informed that he expected a feast to be prepared for him and his company. His messengers transmitted his request to the queen, who was taken by surprise and had no chance to

---

\* Saxland, corresponding roughly with Saxony, was a general term for northern Germany.

gather her forces. Making the best of the situation, she invited King Helgi to a feast along with all his following.

Helgi arrived at the feast and had himself placed in the high seat beside the queen. The two drank together throughout the evening. Nothing was lacking and Queen Olof showed no sign of displeasure. King Helgi said to the queen, 'The situation is this: I want us to drink to our marriage this evening. There are enough people here for such a celebration and tonight we will share one bed.'

She answered, 'It seems to me that this plan has moved too fast. Yet I do not think that I could find a man more courteous than you, if I were of a mind to attach myself to any man.[19] But I certainly do not expect you would want to undertake such a union with dishonour.'

The king replied that it was fitting, because of her pride and arrogance, 'that we remain together for as long as it pleases me'.

She answered, 'I would choose to have more of my friends here, but since I can now do nothing you must decide this matter. And I expect you to behave honourably toward me.'

The drinking continued throughout the evening and long into the night. The queen was so cheerful that no one noticed in her anything other than that she thought well of the marriage. Finally, when Helgi was brought to bed, she was waiting there for him.

The king had drunk so much that at once he fell down asleep onto the bed. Taking advantage of his state, the queen stuck him with a sleep thorn.* When the last of the men had left, the queen got up. She shaved off all his hair and smeared him with tar.

Next, she took a leather sack made for sleeping and placed some clothes in it. After that she grabbed hold of the king and stuffed him into the sack. Then she called her men and had them carry the king to his ships.

The queen next awakened Helgi's men, telling them that their king had gone back to the ships and, because of a favourable wind, was planning to set sail. They jumped up, each one moving as fast as he could, but, drunk and confused, they scarcely knew what to do.

---

* Putting a sleep thorn into a person's ear was thought to produce a charmed sleep from which the person would not awaken until the sleep thorn fell out.

When the men arrived at the ships, the king was nowhere to be found. They did, however, see that a large sack was there. Curious about its contents, they decided to look while waiting for the king. They assumed that he would be coming a little later. When they untied the sack, they found their king, shamefully tricked. The sleep thorn fell away, and the king awoke, though his dreams had not been pleasant. He was now in a vile temper regarding the queen.

But about Queen Olof, there is more to be told: She spent the night gathering her men and there was no lack of numbers. Meanwhile King Helgi could not decide how to get back at her. When he and his men heard from the land the sound of trumpets and the blast of war horns, Helgi realized that it would be best to get away as quickly as possible. As it turned out, a fair wind was blowing at the time. King Helgi sailed home to his kingdom, bearing this dishonour and disgrace. He was filled with resentment about the outcome and often contemplated how to take vengeance on the queen.

## 7. King Helgi's Vengeance

Queen Olof remained now for a time in her kingdom; her arrogance and her overbearing manner had never been greater. After the feast she had offered King Helgi, she kept a strong guard around her. News of their dealings spread far and wide throughout the different lands. Everyone thought it a flagrant misdeed to have mocked such a king in this way.

Not long afterward King Helgi again set sail in his ships. This time he headed toward Saxland, making for the queen's royal residence. The queen had a large force ready, but Helgi landed his ships in a hidden inlet. He told his men to wait for him there until the third day and, if he had not returned by then, to go their own way.

Helgi took with him two chests filled with gold and silver. He obtained some rags which he used for outer clothing. He then made his way to the woods and hid the treasure there.

Next, going toward the queen's hall, he met one of her slaves. He asked the man for news of the country. The thrall said the times were peaceful and good and asked the stranger who he was. Helgi let on that he was a poor beggar.

'All the same,' Helgi said, 'I have found a huge treasure in the forest, and it seems advisable for me to show you where it is.' They went to the woods and he showed the slave the treasure. The slave was much impressed by the value of the treasure, believing that good fortune had struck.

'How greedy is the queen?' asked the beggar.

'She is the greediest of women,' replied the slave.

'Then this treasure will please her,' said the beggar. 'Though I found it, she will think she owns it because it is on her land. Good fortune must not now be turned to bad, so I will not hide this wealth. The queen can decide on my share as she wishes; deciding what will suit me best. But will she take the trouble to come here to get the treasure?'

'I am sure that she will,' answered the slave, 'if it is done secretly.'

'Here,' said the beggar, 'is a necklace and a ring. These I will give to you if you succeed in persuading her to go alone into the woods. On the other hand, I will devise a plan if she becomes angry with you.'

After discussing the matter, they arrived at a bargain. The slave went home and told the queen that he had found a huge cache of treasure in the woods, 'enough,' he said, 'to guarantee the happiness of many men.' He asked her to come with him quickly to retrieve the wealth.

She replied, 'If what you say is true, this story will make your fortune; if not, it will bring death to you. But, since I have discovered you in the past to be reliable, I will trust in what you say.'

Then she showed just how greedy she was. So that no one else would know, she arranged that the two of them would go alone in the dead of night.

But when they came into the forest, Helgi was there waiting. He grabbed hold of the queen and told her that their meeting was an ideal opportunity to avenge his disgrace.

The queen admitted that she had behaved badly toward him; 'But now, I want to make it all up to you, and you shall wed me honourably.'

'No,' he said, 'you will not have that choice. You will come with me to the ships and remain there for as long as it pleases me. For my own pride's sake I must take some vengeance on you after the ugly and shameful way you toyed with me.'

'For now,' she said, 'you are the one who will decide.' The king then slept with the queen for many nights.

Then the queen returned home. As just told, Helgi wreaked his vengeance on her, and now she became profoundly unhappy with her lot. King Helgi continued on his voyage, bringing war to others and acquiring fame.


## The Girl Yrsa

After some time, Queen Olof gave birth to a child. It was a girl. The queen treated the child with complete neglect. She had a dog named Yrsa; she called the little girl after it, so that the child came to be named Yrsa.[20] She was a beautiful child, but when she was twelve years old she was sent to tend the herd. The girl was told only that she was the daughter of a poor farmer and his elderly wife. The deceit was possible because the queen had concealed her condition so well that only a few people knew that she had given birth.

So matters continued until the girl was thirteen. Then King Helgi returned to Olof's lands and, curious to know what had happened there, he put on beggar's clothes. He saw a large herd in a forest tended by a young woman. She was so beautiful that he thought he had never seen a more lovely woman. He asked her name and inquired about her family and kinship. She answered, 'I am the daughter of a poor man and am called Yrsa.'

'Your eyes are not those of a servant,' he said, and suddenly feelings of love welled up in him. He said it would be proper for a beggar to marry her, because she was a poor man's daughter.

Although she asked him not to do this; he took her with him back to the ships and sailed home to his kingdom.

When Queen Olof learned what had happened, she behaved deceitfully. In public she pretended to have no knowledge of the situation. In her private thoughts, however, she calculated that these events would bring grief and dishonour to King Helgi and that neither success nor joy would come of them. King Helgi married Yrsa and loved her very much.

## The Ring

A ring owned by King Helgi was a widely famed treasure. Both brothers wanted it, and so too did their sister Signy. King Hroar once paid a visit to the kingdom of his brother King Helgi, who prepared a magnificent feast in Hroar's honour.

King Hroar said, 'Between us, you are the greater man. I have settled in Northumberland and therefore am now willing to grant you my share of the kingdom that we own jointly. I will make this agreement if you will share with me some of our treasured possessions. I want the ring, the one that is the best treasure in your possession and that both of us would like to own.'

'Brother,' said Helgi, 'after such a speech, nothing else is fitting but that you should have the ring.'

King Hroar returned home to his kingdom and remained there in peace.

## 8. *Jarl Hrok Claims King Hroar's Ring*

Next came the news that Jarl Saevil had died and that his son Hrok had then assumed rule. Hrok was a cruel and exceptionally greedy man.

His mother often described the ring owned by her brothers. 'To my mind, it would be proper,' she said, 'if they remembered us with a grant of some form of wealth. We supported them when they were taking vengeance for our father, yet they have not rewarded us for our help either in respect to your father or in respect to me.'

Hrok agreed: 'What you say is plain as day; the situation is disgraceful. I will go to them and find out what they are willing to do in order to satisfy our honour.' Hrok then set off to meet King Helgi. He demanded a third of the Danish kingdom or the great ring. He did not know that Hroar had the ring in his possession.

King Helgi said, 'You make bold demands and act with arrogance. We won the kingdom with our courage, staking our lives on the outcome. We acted with the support of your father and of my foster father Regin. Other good men also aided us. We will certainly reward you because of our kinship; that is, if you are willing to consent to our proposal. This kingdom has, however, cost me so much that I am by no means willing to lose it. Furthermore, King Hroar has now assumed ownership of the ring, and I doubt that it will be available to you.'

Hrok left very dissatisfied. Next he sought out King Hroar, who received him with honour. Hrok stayed with Hroar for a time. Once, while sailing down the coast, they put in at a fjord. Hrok said, 'It seems to me, kinsman, that it would be worthy of your honour if you placed the great ring under my control. By doing so you will dignify our kinship.'

The king responded, 'I have given so much to get this ring that I will by no means part with it.'

Hrok said, 'Then you must allow me to look at it, as I am very curious to know whether the ring is as much of a treasure as is claimed.'

'That is a small thing to do for you,' said Hroar, 'and I will certainly let you look at it.' He then produced the ring for Hrok to see.

For a while Hrok studied the ring, declaring finally that there was no possibility of exaggeration when describing it. 'I have never seen a comparable treasure, and the reason you esteem the ring so highly is obvious. The best solution, it seems to me, is that neither of us, or, for that matter, anyone else should enjoy it.' He then threw the ring as far out as he could into the sea.

King Hroar said, 'You are a thoroughly odious man.' He then ordered Hrok's foot chopped off and sent him back to his kingdom. Hrok soon recovered his health, and even the stump of his leg healed. Then he assembled troops with the intention of avenging his shameful injury. He gathered a large force and arrived with stealth in Northumberland. At the time King Hroar was feasting with only a few followers, and Hrok attacked at once. A hard-fought battle ensued, but the sides were uneven and King Hroar was killed.

Hrok finished his conquest of the kingdom and had himself given the title of king. Next he asked to marry Ogn, the daughter of King Nordri and the wife of his uncle, King Hroar. King Nordri thus found himself thrust into a grim dilemma, especially because he was then an old man and hardly fit for fighting. He told his daughter Ogn how matters stood, stating that, despite his age, he would not refuse to give battle, if that was her wish.

She answered with deep sorrow, 'Of course this union is against my will. I see, however, that your life hangs in the balance, and so I will not reject him. But some delay must be arranged, for I am carrying a child, and this is the matter that must be attended to first. King Hroar is the father.'

The request was put to Hrok. He was willing to grant a delay if by doing so he could more easily secure both the kingdom and the marriage. It seemed to Hrok that he had greatly advanced himself on this journey, having brought about the downfall of so famous and powerful a king.

Seizing the opportunity, Ogn sent messengers to King Helgi with instructions to tell him that she would not get into a bed with Hrok, that is, if the choice were hers and she were not being forced: 'The reason is that I am carrying King Hroar's child.' The messengers set off and repeated her words just as they had been told.

King Helgi responded that it 'was wisely said on her part, because I will avenge my brother Hroar.' Hrok, however, suspected nothing.

## 9. Vengeance and King Hroar's Son Agnar

Queen Ogn next gave birth to a son named Agnar, who from early on was big and full of promise. When King Helgi heard this news, he gathered his forces and set out to fight Hrok. The battle that followed ended with Hrok's capture.

King Helgi said to Hrok: 'You are a thoroughly vile chieftain, but I will not kill you. Instead, it will shame you more to live with pain and torment.' Then he had Hrok's legs and arms broken and sent him back to his kingdom. Hrok was utterly ruined.

When Agnar, Hroar's son, was twelve years old, men thought they had never seen any man his equal. He was foremost in all accomplishments and he became a great warrior. He became so famous that, when old tales are told, he is widely held to be the greatest of champions, past or present.

Agnar inquired about the location of the fjord into which Hrok had thrown the ring. Many people had searched for the ring, using all kinds of methods, but the ring was never found.

Agnar sailed his ship into the fjord, saying that it 'would be a great feat to snare the ring, if only someone knew the bearings'. After being told where the ring had been thrown into the sea, Agnar got ready and dived into the deep. He surfaced, but without the ring. He went down under for a second time, but again did not find the ring. After saying that 'it has been sought after carelessly', he went down a third time and came up with the ring.

Agnar gained widespread fame from this exploit; his reputation now exceeded his father's.[21]

King Helgi stayed at home in his kingdom during the winters, but in the summers he went out raiding. He became a famous man, more renowned than his father. He and Yrsa loved each other deeply. They had one son. He was named Hrolf, the one who later became a most worthy man.[22]

## 10. *King Helgi and Queen Yrsa*

Queen Olof learned that King Helgi and Yrsa loved each other dearly and were content with their marriage. The news displeased her, and she set out to pay them a visit. When she reached their lands, she sent word to Queen Yrsa, and the women met. Yrsa invited Olof to accompany her home to the hall. Queen Olof replied that she did not wish to do so. She explained that she had no honour to repay to King Helgi.

Yrsa said, 'You behaved shamefully to me when I was with you. Do you have anything to tell me about my family? Who are they? I suspect that I am not the daughter of a serving man and a common woman, as I was told.' In reply, Olof said: 'It is likely that I can tell you something about your parentage. My main reason for coming here was to tell you what I know about it. But are you well content with your marriage?'

'Yes,' she replied, 'and well I might be, because I am married to the most noble and most famous of kings.'

'Your contentment may not be as secure as you think,' said Olof, 'for he is your father, and you are my daughter.'

Yrsa said, 'I have, I am sure, the worst and cruellest of mothers. What you are telling me is so monstrous that it will never be forgotten.'

'You have suffered,' Olof said, 'from Helgi's actions and my anger. Now I invite you to come home with me. You will receive honour and esteem, and I will behave toward you as best I can in every respect.'

Yrsa answered, 'I have no idea what that will bring, but I do know that I cannot stay here, aware as I am of the shame that darkens this place.' She then went to King Helgi, telling him how oppressive her situation now was.

The king said, 'You have a cruel enough mother, but I want things to continue as they are now.' But she argued that things could not continue as they were and that, from now on, they must no longer live together.

Yrsa then went with Queen Olof and stayed in Saxland for a time.

King Helgi suffered so deeply because of his wife's departure that, grievously unhappy, he took to his bed.

No match was thought better than one with Yrsa, but kings were slow in asking for her hand. The main reason was the possibility that King Helgi would in the end come after her, enraged that she had married another man.

## 11. *The Elfin Woman and the Birth of Skuld*

There was a king named Adils; he was powerful and greedy.[23] From his stronghold at Uppsala, he ruled over Sweden. King Adils heard of Yrsa and prepared his ships, setting out to ask for an audience with Olof and Yrsa. Olof prepared a feast in honour of King Adils, regaling him with all manner of refinement and courtesy. King Adils asked for Queen Yrsa's hand in marriage.

Olof said, 'You must have heard about her situation. If she agrees to marry you, I will not oppose your request.' So Adils presented his suit to Yrsa. She responded, telling him that his chance of success was not good, 'because you are an unpopular king'.

Nevertheless the suit went forward. Yrsa was uncommitted either way, and it mattered little whether she said more or less concerning the proposal. But finally she accompanied King Adils when he sailed off. King Helgi was not notified, because Adils thought himself the more prominent of the two kings. King Helgi did not even know what had happened until after the couple arrived in Sweden, where King Adils had a splendid wedding feast prepared for Yrsa. It was news of this celebration that finally reached Helgi, who became twice as unhappy as before. King Helgi slept alone in a small detached building. So matters continued for a while. Olof is now out of the saga.

It is said that one Yule evening King Helgi was in bed.[24] The weather outside was foul, yet someone came to the door, tapping weakly on it. It occurred to Helgi that it was unkingly for him to allow any person, however wretched, to remain outside when he could help. So the king got up and opened the door. He saw someone or something, poor and tattered, standing outside.

After saying, 'You have done well, King,' it came into the room.

The king said, 'Take some straw and a bearskin for yourself so that you will not freeze.'

The visitor said, 'Let me into your bed, Sire. I want to sleep next to you, for my life is at stake.'

The king replied, 'You repel me, but if it is as you say, then lie down here along the side of the bed. Keep your clothes on, and I will not come to any harm.'

She did as the king asked, and he turned away from her. A light was burning in the house, and after a time, he glanced over his shoulder at her. What he saw was a sleeping woman so fair that he thought he had never seen anyone so beautiful. She was dressed in a silken gown. Quickly and tenderly, he turned toward her.

She said, 'Now I will leave. You have released me from a terrible bondage, which was my stepmother's curse. I have visited many kings, but none of them accepted me because of my looks. I do not want to stay here any longer.'

'No,' said the king, 'there is no possibility that you may leave so soon. We will not part that way. I will arrange a quick wedding for us, because you please me well.'

She said, 'You are the one to make the decision, my lord.' And so that night they slept together.

In the morning she spoke to him, saying, 'We have slept together because of your lust, and you will know that we will have a child. Do now as I tell you, King. Visit our child next winter at this same time down at your ships' landing. Unless you do so, you will pay for it.' After this, she went away.

The king was now somewhat happier than before.

Time passed and Helgi forgot, giving no thought to the warning. But after three winters, there is this to tell: At midnight three people came riding up to the same house in which the king was sleeping. They brought a girl-child with them and put her down outside the house.

Then the woman, who was holding the child, said, 'You must

know, King, that your kinsmen will pay for your ignoring my request. Nevertheless, you will reap a benefit from having released me from the curse. Be aware that the girl is named Skuld, and she is our daughter.'* Then the people rode away.

Skuld's mother was an elfin woman,[25] and the king never again saw or heard of her. Skuld grew up with the king; from an early age she showed a vicious temperament.

It is said that King Helgi prepared to set out on a voyage to forget his sorrow. Hrolf, his son, stayed behind. King Helgi raided far and wide, performing great deeds.

## 12. *King Adils and King Helgi Meet*

Meanwhile, King Adils remained at Uppsala. He had twelve berserkers, who defended his land against all dangers and attack.[26] King Helgi prepared his voyage to Uppsala to retrieve Yrsa. When King Adils learned that Helgi had landed, he asked the queen how she wished to have King Helgi received.

Queen Yrsa answered, 'You will decide that for yourself, but you know from before that there is no man whom, because of our relationship, I am more bound to support.'

King Adils thought it fitting to invite Helgi to a feast, but he had no intention for the meeting to occur without treachery. Accepting the invitation, King Helgi travelled to the feast with one hundred men, leaving most of his followers with the ships.

King Adils received Helgi with open arms. Queen Yrsa, hoping to reconcile the two kings, showed all honour toward King Helgi. For his part, Helgi was so pleased to see the queen that he let everything else slip by him, for he wanted to make use of all the available time to talk with her. And so they sat down to the feast.

Then King Adils' berserkers returned home. As soon as they had

* *Skuld* means a debt or a payment due. The name is also used in the *Prose Edda* for one of the three Norns.

landed, King Adils met them secretly. He ordered the berserkers to hide in the woods between the fortress and King Helgi's ships. From there the berserkers were to ambush King Helgi when he returned to his ships. 'I will send reinforcements to help you. My troops will attack them in the rear, and in this way Helgi and his men will be caught in the claws of a trap. My intention is to attack Helgi so that he cannot escape. I can see that he is so much in love with the queen that I dare not risk whatever he is planning.'

As King Helgi sat at the feast, the treachery was carefully concealed from both him and the queen. Queen Yrsa asked King Adils to give Helgi splendid gifts at their parting. Adils complied by giving Helgi gold as well as treasured articles, intending, in fact, to enjoy them himself.

When King Helgi then set out, King Adils and the queen accompanied him on his way, and the queen and the kings parted on seemingly friendly terms. Not long after King Adils had turned back, King Helgi and his men became aware of an impending attack, and soon a battle started. King Helgi pushed forward, fighting valiantly, but he and his men faced overwhelming odds. Having suffered great wounds, King Helgi fell there after gaining renown. Some of King Adils' forces had attacked from the rear, and Helgi and his men had found themselves caught as though between hammer and anvil.

Queen Yrsa learned about these events only after King Helgi had fallen and the battle ended. With King Helgi fell all the followers who had accompanied him to the feast. The rest of Helgi's men fled home to Denmark.

Here ends the tale of King Helgi.

## 13. *King Adils' Pride and Queen Yrsa's Displeasure*

King Adils became boastful and arrogant about his victory. It seemed to him that he had greatly distinguished himself, having overcome a king as important and famous as Helgi. But Queen Yrsa said, 'It is hardly fitting to boast so much, even if you have tricked that man to whom I owed the greatest obligation, and the one I loved the most. For the same reason I will never be loyal to you if you fight his kinsmen. I plan to put your berserkers to death as soon as I can, that is, if I find someone manly enough to do so, both for my sake and as proof of his own worth.'

King Adils asked her not to threaten him or his berserkers, 'because it will not help you. But I do want to compensate you for the death of your father. If you will accept it, I will give you magnificent gifts, including both riches and valuable possessions.'

The queen, appeased by this offer, accepted redress from the king. Nevertheless from then on she was of an uneasy temper, often watching for a chance to harm or to disgrace the berserkers. After the fall of King Helgi, the queen never exhibited joy or good humour. Now, more than before, disagreements arose in the hall. If she could find a way to avoid it, the queen chose not to submit to King Adils' will.

King Adils believed that he had made himself exceedingly famous, and now all those who served among his followers and his champions thought themselves masterly men. King Adils remained at home in his kingdom, convinced that no one would raise a shield in opposition to his authority or dare to test the strength of his berserkers.

King Adils was a devoted sacrificer and a man full of sorcery.[27]

## 14. *Svipdag and the Berserkers*

A farmer was named Svip. He lived in Sweden, far away from other men. He was wealthy and had been a great champion. At times Svip was not all that he seemed to be, for he was deeply learned in many arts, including magic. Svip had three sons, who are named here. One was called Svipdag,[28] another Beygad and the third, the eldest, was called Hvitserk.[29] They were all imposing men, strong and handsome.

One day, when Svipdag was eighteen years old, he said to his father, 'Our life up here in the mountains is dismal. We live in remote valleys and unpopulated regions; we never visit other people, nor do others come to see us. We would be more enterprising if we went to King

Adils and joined his company of followers and champions, if he would accept us.'

Svip replied, 'Your suggestion seems ill-advised to me. King Adils is a cruel man and, although he can act in a pleasing manner, he is not trustworthy. His men, although impressive, are filled with envy. Yet this king is certainly a powerful and famous man.'

Svipdag answered, 'Men must try, if they are to advance. Without effort, no one learns which way luck will turn. I do not want to stay here any longer, whatever else lies in my future.'

And when it was clear that Svipdag was determined to leave, his father gave him a great axe, a handsome and dangerous weapon. Svip then counselled his son, 'Do not envy others and avoid arrogance, for such conduct diminishes one's fame. Defend yourself if you are attacked. It is becoming to be humble, yet at the same time you must make a bold showing if put to a test.'[30] He outfitted Svipdag with fine armour, giving him also other gear and a good horse.

Svipdag rode off. Arriving one evening at King Adils' stronghold, he saw the men taking part in games in front of the hall.[31] The king was sitting nearby on a large golden chair with his berserkers close beside him.

When Svipdag arrived at the stockade, he found the gate to the fortress locked. It was the custom to ask permission before riding in, but Svipdag paid no heed to this procedure. He broke down the gate and rode into the courtyard.

The king said, 'This man proceeds with less concern for proper conduct than has ever been attempted here before. He may be a powerful individual who does not mind being put to the test.'

The berserkers immediately began to scowl, for to them Svipdag seemed to have behaved arrogantly. Svipdag rode up to the king and greeted him well, for he knew how to do so skilfully.

When the king asked the newcomer who he was, Svipdag gave his own name and then named his father. The king recognized him at once, and everybody believed him to be a great warrior, a man of exceptional talent.

Meanwhile the game continued. Svipdag sat on a log and watched the contest. The berserkers looked menacingly at him and told the king that they wanted to test him.

The king answered, 'I think that he is no weakling, still it seems to me a good idea to test him to see whether he is as much a man as he thinks he is.'

Men now crowded into the hall. The berserkers went up to Svipdag, asking him whether he was a champion, as he behaved so arrogantly. Svipdag answered that he was the equal of any one of them, a reply that increased their anger and heightened their desire to fight. Yet, the king told them to remain quiet for the evening.

The berserkers, however, grimaced and bellowed. They said to Svipdag, 'Do you dare to fight us? If so, you will need more than big words and a scornful manner. We will test whatever strength is in you.'

Svipdag answered, 'I agree to fight, but with only one man at a time. In this way, we will see how many others among you want to take their turn.'

The king was pleased that they wanted to test themselves, and the queen said, 'This man is welcome here.'

The berserkers answered her, 'We already know that you want us all dead in Hel, but we are too strong to fall because of mere words or ill will.'

The queen said there was nothing wrong in the king's wish to find out how much support he has 'where you are concerned, since he trusts so much in you'.

The leader of the berserkers answered the queen, 'I will block your wishes and curb your haughtiness in a way that will leave us nothing to fear from this man.'

The next morning a fierce single combat took place.[32] The blows struck were powerful, and everyone realized that the newcomer's sword cut with great strength. As the first berserker fell back before the newcomer, Svipdag killed him. At once a second berserker stepped forward, set on vengeance, but he suffered the same treatment. Svipdag did not cease until he had killed four of the berserkers.

Then King Adils said, 'You have caused me grave injury and now you will pay for it.' He ordered his men to attack and kill Svipdag. Meanwhile the queen, intending to save Svipdag, had assembled her supporters. She told the king that he ought to realize that Svipdag alone had more excellence than all the berserkers together.

The queen effected a truce, and it seemed to all that Svipdag was a man of exceptional valour. Now upon the advice of Queen Yrsa, Svipdag was seated on a bench directly across from the king.

Later, as it grew dark, Svipdag began to survey the area, for it seemed to him that he had not sufficiently harmed the berserkers. He decided to goad them into yet another fight, thinking it likely that they would attack him, if they saw him alone. As expected, they started to fight at once. After they had been fighting for a while, the king arrived and separated them.

The king then outlawed the remaining berserkers, because all together they could not overcome one lone man. The king said he had not known that they were so feeble, because they excelled when it came to boasting. The berserkers were forced to leave, and they threatened to raid the king's territory. The king seemed unconcerned with their threats, declaring that these she-dogs had no courage in them.

The berserkers, disgraced and dishonoured, now left. In truth, it was the king who had first urged them to attack and kill Svipdag when they saw him leaving the hall by himself. Had they done so, they would have avenged themselves without the queen's knowledge. Svipdag, however, had already killed one of the berserkers by the time the king arrived to separate them.

The king requested that Svipdag support him no less strongly than all the berserkers had done previously. 'All the more,' the king said, 'because the queen wants you to replace the berserkers.'

Svipdag now remained there for a time.

Not long afterward, news of war reached the king. The berserkers, having gathered a large force, were raiding his territory. He then asked Svipdag to go against the berserkers, calling it his duty. The king said he was prepared to raise for Svipdag as large a force as necessary. But Svipdag did not want to lead the army; instead he wanted to serve the king, following him wherever he went. The king, however, was adamant that Svipdag be the leader.

Svipdag replied, 'Then I want you to grant me the lives of twelve men, whenever I decide on it.'

The king promised, 'This, I will grant you.' Then Svipdag set out for battle; the king, however, remained at home. Svipdag ordered 'war-spurs' to be made, and these spikes were to be used against horses.[33] He spread them on the ground where the battlefield was marked and also prepared the field with other stratagems. Then a fierce battle began.

The Vikings* at first reeled back, suffering cruelly from the spikes. One berserker was killed, along with a large part of the invading force. Those raiders still alive fled to their ships and escaped.

Svipdag, having the victory to boast of, returned to the king. The king thanked him well for his bravery and for his defence of the land.

Queen Yrsa said, 'Certainly that seat is better occupied with a hero such as Svipdag than with your berserkers.' The king agreed.

Those berserkers who had escaped once again gathered a following and returned to raid King Adils' kingdom. As before, the king challenged Svipdag to go against them, promising to supply him with a fine troop of warriors. Svipdag prepared for battle, even though he had a third fewer men than the berserkers. The king, however, promised to join him with his own bodyguard, and Svipdag set out sooner than the berserkers had expected. The two sides soon clashed, fighting a hard battle.

Meanwhile King Adils assembled his force, intending to surprise the berserkers from the rear.

Now we return to farmer Svip. He awoke suddenly from his sleep, sighed deeply and said to his sons, 'Your brother Svipdag is in need of your support. He is engaging in a battle not far from here and has by far the smaller force. He has lost one of his eyes[34] and has suffered many wounds. Although he has killed three berserkers, another three are still fighting.'

The brothers quickly armed themselves and set off for the battle-

---

* The saga calls the raiding berserkers Vikings (*vikingar*). In Old Norse the term is used to describe pirates or raiders in general. The medieval Scandinavians did not, as is popularly done today, use the word as an ethnic term.

ground, where the Vikings had twice as many men as Svipdag. By then, Svipdag had accomplished much, but he was sorely wounded and had lost one eye. Also, many of his followers had been killed. The king still had not come to his aid.

Arriving at the battlefield, the brothers entered into the fighting. They pushed resolutely forward until they were opposite the berserkers. Now they finished the contest, and all the berserkers were felled by the brothers. With the tide of battle changing, the death toll mounted in the ranks of the Vikings. Those, however, among the berserkers' men who chose to accept their lives from the brothers, swore allegiance to them.

Then the brothers went to the king to tell him what had happened. The king thanked them well for the impressive victory. Svipdag had two arm wounds, a large head wound and was one-eyed for the rest of his life. For a time he lay disabled by these wounds, the queen nursing him.

After regaining his health, Svipdag told the king he was planning to leave: 'I want to look for a king who will honour us more than you do. You have rewarded me poorly for defending your land and for our winning so great a victory for you.'

King Adils appealed to Svipdag to remain with him. He promised to do full well by the brothers, declaring that no one would be valued more than they. Svipdag, however, wanted only to ride away, mainly because the king, undecided about whether he wanted Svipdag or the berserkers to win the victory, had not come to the battlefield before the fighting had ended. The whole time the king had watched the contest from the woods and could have joined in whenever he chose. In fact, to the king it would have made no difference if Svipdag had been defeated and lay with his face in the dirt.

## 15. *Svipdag and His Brothers Join King Hrolf's Men*

The brothers prepared to leave and nothing could stop them. The king asked where they intended to go, but they said they had not yet decided on a plan. 'Right now, we will just leave. I want to learn the ways of other kings and not grow old here in Sweden.' They thanked the queen graciously for the honour she had shown to Svipdag and went to their horses.

Mounting their horses, they rode out and finally arrived back at their father's place. They wanted his advice about what tasks they should now undertake.

Svip said that in his opinion the greatest renown was to be had in joining King Hrolf and his champions in Denmark: 'There you are most likely to find a way to distinguish yourselves, while quenching your thirst for violence and your greed for fame. I have had trustworthy reports that the most formidable champions from the northern lands have assembled there.'

Svipdag asked, 'What is King Hrolf like?' His father answered, 'I have heard that King Hrolf is open-handed and generous and so trustworthy and particular about his friends that his equal cannot be found. He withholds neither gold nor treasure from nearly everyone who wants or needs them. He is handsome in looks, powerful in deeds and a worthy opponent. The fairest of men, Hrolf is fierce with the greedy, yet gentle and accommodating with the unpretentious and modest. Toward all those who do not threaten him, he is the most humble of men, responding with equal mildness to both the powerful and the poor. Hrolf is so great that his name will not be forgotten as long as the world remains inhabited. He has exacted tribute from all kings who are near him, for everyone is willing to serve him.'

Svipdag said, 'After hearing your report, father, I and all my brothers are determined to serve King Hrolf, if he will accept us.'

Farmer Svip said, 'You must decide for yourself about your travels and other affairs, but I would like you to stay home with me.'

The brothers said there was no hope of that. Then they wished their father and mother a good life and set off on their way, journeying until they reached King Hrolf.

Svipdag went immediately before the king and greeted him. King Hrolf asked who the newcomer was. Svipdag then gave the king his name and the names of all the brothers, saying that they had been for a time with King Adils.

The king replied, 'Why, then, have you come here? There is no love lost between us and Adils' men.'

Svipdag responded, 'I know that, Lord. Nevertheless, if it is possible, I and all my brothers want to become your men, though we might seem to you to be of little significance.'

The king answered, 'I had never intended to make friends among King Adils' men. But, because you have approached me first, I will receive you. I can guess that the man who does not refuse you has the best of the bargain, because I see that you and your companions are admirable warriors. I heard that you have won much fame in killing King Adils' berserkers and accomplishing many other feats.'

'Where do you want us to sit?' asked Svipdag.

The king replied, 'Sit next to the man called Bjalki, but leave enough room farther in on the benches for twelve men.'

Before leaving King Adils, Svipdag had promised to return to him, but now the brothers went to the seats assigned them by King Hrolf. Svipdag asked Bjalki why space was being saved farther in from them. Bjalki said that the king's twelve berserkers always sat there when they came home. At that moment they were still out fighting.

Skur was the name of one of King Hrolf's daughters; another, called Drifa, was now at home with the king. Drifa, the most courteous of women, showed kindness to the brothers, making life altogether more pleasant for them.

So the situation continued throughout the summer, until the berserkers returned to the king's guard in the fall. According to their custom, when the berserkers entered the hall they confronted each man in turn. The leader of the berserkers stood, asking each man seated before him if he reckoned himself as an equal. In reply, the king's men tried to find different expressions, which they regarded as either the most fitting or the least dishonourable. It could be felt that everyone thought himself sorely lacking in being the equal of the berserkers.

Then the berserkers' leader came to Svipdag, asking whether he thought himself an equal. Svipdag leapt up and drew his sword, claiming that he was in no way less than the berserker.

The berserker replied, 'Then strike at my helmet.' Svipdag did so but his sword did not cut into the helmet. The two men then got ready to fight.

King Hrolf, quickly positioning himself between the two, forbade their fighting. He said that they should be called equal from now on, declaring them 'both my friends'. Thus the two, accepting equality, were reconciled. From that time on they were always in agreement, standing together in war and winning victory wherever they went.

King Hrolf sent men to Sweden to meet with Queen Yrsa, his mother. He requested her to send him the treasure that had belonged to King Helgi, his father. King Adils had taken this treasure for himself when King Helgi was killed.

Yrsa said it would be proper for her to arrange this matter with King Adils, if only she could. 'If you yourself seek the treasure, my son, then I will be faithful to you in this matter, but King Adils is so greedy a man that he never cares how he comes by his wealth.' She asked that her reply be given to King Hrolf and, along with her message, she sent him costly gifts.

## 16. *King Hrolf Tricks King Hjorvard*

Because King Hrolf was out raiding, his encounter with King Adils was delayed. With the large force he had assembled, Hrolf succeeded in making all the kings he fought pay tribute to him. A deciding factor was that all the best warriors wanted to be in his following. They chose to serve Hrolf, because he was far more generous with rewards than any of the other kings.

King Hrolf had established the seat of his kingdom at a place in Denmark called Hleidargard,[35] where his fortress was large and strong. He and his followers lived lavishly, and there was more splendour at Hleidargard than at any other noble establishment known at the time.

Hjorvard was the name of a powerful king.[36] He married Skuld, the sister of King Hrolf. The arrangement had been made with the consent of King Adils, Queen Yrsa and King Hrolf, her brother.

Some time later, King Hrolf invited his brother-in-law, King

Hjorvard, to a feast. One day during the festivities, the two kings found themselves standing together outside. King Hrolf unfastened his belt and, while doing so, he handed his sword to King Hjorvard to hold.

When King Hrolf had fastened his belt again, he took back his sword, saying to King Hjorvard, 'We both know the old adage that he who holds the sword of a man who is undoing his belt, will from then on be the lesser of the two. Therefore, you are now a king under my rule and you must endure this status as patiently as the others do.'

Hjorvard became enraged at this but nonetheless was obliged to let it stand. He went home with matters as they were, but he was little pleased with his lot. Despite his discontent, he delivered his tribute to King Hrolf, acting just like Hrolf's other underkings, who showed obedience.

And here ends the story of Svipdag.

## 17. *King Hring of Norway Marries Hvit*

It is said that to the north in Norway a king named Hring ruled over Uppdales.[37] He had a son named Bjorn.[38] It is told that the queen died, and the king and many others found this a great loss. Hring's countrymen and counsellors asked him to remarry, and so he sent men to the south seeking a wife. But strong headwinds and powerful storms forced them to turn their prows around, letting the ships run before the wind. So it happened that driven by the wind, they were forced north to Finnmark, where they remained for the winter.[39]

One day they went onshore. They walked inland and came to a house. Inside sat two beautiful women, who received them well. The women asked them where they had come from, and the king's men gave an account of their journey and explained their errand. They asked the women about themselves, inquiring why women so beautiful and refined were there alone, so far from other people.

The older woman answered, 'For everything, friends, there is a reason. We are here because a powerful king asked for my daughter's

34

THE LOVE OF BERA AND BJORN

hand. Because she did not want to marry him, he threatened her with rough treatment. So I am keeping her here in this secret hiding place while her father is away at war.'

They asked who her father might be.

'She is the daughter of the King of the Lapps,' said the woman.

The men asked for their names.

The older woman replied, 'I am called Ingebjorg and my daughter is named Hvit.* I am the Lapp king's mistress.'

A girl was there to serve them. The king's men, much taken with these women, decided to ask whether Hvit would go back with them and marry King Hring. The man in charge of the king's mission brought up the question. Hvit did not respond quickly; instead, she deferred the issue to her mother's consideration.

'As the old saying goes,' said her mother, 'out of every trouble comes some gain. But it displeases me that we are making this arrangement without first asking her father's consent. Nevertheless, it must be ventured, if Hvit is to get ahead.'

Hvit then prepared herself to go with them, and they started on the journey to King Hring. The messengers at once inquired whether the king wanted to marry the woman or if she should be sent back. The king, well pleased with the woman, married her at once. He was not concerned that she was neither rich nor powerful. At this time, the king was getting on in years, and the effects of his age were soon apparent in the queen's behaviour.

## 18. *The Love of Bera and Bjorn*

A freeman's farm lay a short distance from the king's estate. The farmer had a wife and one daughter, who was named Bera.[40] She was young and lovely to look at. Bjorn, the king's son, and Bera, the freeman's daughter, had played together as children, and the two were very close. The freeman was wealthy; he had long been out raiding and in his

---

* *Hvit* means white.

BJORN REJECTS QUEEN HVIT'S ADVANCES: THE CURSE

youth had been a great champion. Bera and Bjorn loved each other deeply and they often met.

Time passed and nothing noteworthy took place. Bjorn, the king's son, matured to manhood. He grew large and strong; he was well bred and was accomplished in all skills. When King Hring was away at war for long periods, which frequently happened, Hvit stayed at home and governed the land. She was not well liked by the people; toward Bjorn, however, she was gentle and tender, though he paid no heed.

One time when the king was about to set out from home, the queen suggested that Bjorn should stay home to help her govern the land. The king thought that her proposal was advisable. The queen was now becoming overbearing and arrogant. The king told his son Bjorn to stay at home and watch over the kingdom with the queen. Bjorn replied that he had little liking for this idea and that he liked the queen even less. The king then told Bjorn to remain behind, and he then set out with a large force.

## 19. *Bjorn Rejects Queen Hvit's Advances: The Curse*

Bjorn went back to his quarters after arguing with his father, each thinking the other to be wrong. Bjorn, downcast and angry, his face as red as blood, then took to his bed. The queen, wanting to lift his spirits, spoke tenderly to him. He asked her to go away, which she did for a time.

The queen often spoke with Bjorn, telling him that, while the king was away, they had an opportunity to share one bed. She said that their living together would be much better than her experience with a man as old as King Hring.

Bjorn, taking this proposal badly, gave the queen a hard slap. He told her to leave him alone and then threw her out. She said that she was unaccustomed to being rejected or beaten. 'And it seems that you, Bjorn, think it preferable to embrace a commoner's daughter. You deserve a punishment, something far more disgraceful than enjoyment of my love and my tenderness. It would not come as a surprise if something should happen to make you suffer for your stubbornness and your stupidity.'

She then struck him with her wolfskin gloves,[41] telling him to become a cave bear, grim and savage: 'You will eat no food other than your own father's livestock and, in feeding yourself, you will kill more than has ever been observed before. You will never be released from the spell, and your awareness of this disgrace will be more dreadful to you than no remembrance at all.'

## 20. *Bjorn's Transformation into a Bear and the Birth of Bodvar*

Then Bjorn disappeared, and no one knew what had become of him. When people realized that Bjorn was missing, they searched for him. As might have been expected, he was not to be found.

Next to be told is that the king's cattle were being killed in large numbers by a grey bear, large and fierce. One evening it happened that Bera, the freeman's daughter, saw the savage bear. It approached her unthreateningly. She thought she recognized in the bear the eyes[42] of Bjorn, the king's son, and so she did not try to run away. The beast then moved away from her, but she followed it all the way until it came to a cave.

When she entered the cave, a man was standing there. He greeted Bera, the freeman's daughter, and she recognized that he was Bjorn, Hring's son. Theirs was a joyful reunion. For a time they stayed together in the cave, because she did not want to part from him while she still had a choice. He told her it was not right for her to be there with him, because he was a beast by day, even if he again became a man at night.

King Hring, when he returned home from the wars, was told everything that had happened while he was away. He learned about the disappearance of his son Bjorn. He was also told about the huge creature that had arrived in the land, attacking mostly the king's own livestock. The queen strongly urged killing the animal, but this was delayed for a time. The king expressed no opinion, even though he thought the events most unusual.

One night, while Bera and the prince lay in their bed, Bjorn began to speak, 'I suspect that tomorrow will be my death's day, for they will hunt and trap me. In truth, I find no pleasure in living because of the curse that lies upon me. You are my only delight, but that too will now cease. I want to give you the ring that is under my left arm. Tomorrow you will see the men stalking me. When I am dead, go to the king and ask him to give you whatever is under the beast's left shoulder; he will grant you this request.

'The queen,' Bjorn continued, 'will be suspicious of you when you want to leave. She will try to make you eat some of the bear's meat, but you must not eat it, because, as you well know, you are pregnant and will give birth to three boys. They are ours, and it will be obvious from their appearance if you have eaten any of the bear's meat. This queen is a great troll.[43] Then go home to your father, where you will give birth to the boys, one of whom will seem best to you. If you are not able to raise them at home, because of their strange and uncontrollable natures, bring them here to the cave. You will find here a chest with three bottoms. Runes[44] are carved on it, and they will tell what each of the boys should receive as his inheritance. Three weapons are imbedded in the rock, and each of our sons shall have the one intended for him. Our firstborn will be called Elk-Frodi,[45] the second son, Thorir, and the third, Bodvar.[46] It seems to me most likely that they will not be weaklings and that their names will long be remembered.'

Bjorn foretold many things to her, and afterwards the bear-shape came over him. Then the bear went out, and she followed him.

When she looked around, she saw a great company of men circling the side of the mountain. A large pack of hounds raced in front of the men, and now the bear began to run. Turning away from the cave, he ran along the slope of the mountain. The hounds and the king's men gave chase, but the bear proved difficult for them to catch. Before he was overtaken he maimed many men and killed all the dogs.

At last the men formed a ring around him. The bear ranged about inside the ring, but understood the situation and knew that he would not be able to escape. Then he attacked in the direction of the king.

Grabbing the man who stood next to the king, he ripped the man apart while still alive. By then the bear was so exhausted that he threw himself down on the ground. The men seized the opportunity and quickly killed him.

The freeman's daughter saw these events. She went up to the king and said, 'Sire, will you give me what is under the beast's left shoulder?'

The king granted her request, saying that nothing there could be unsuitable to give to her. By then, the king's men were well along in flaying the bear. Bera went to the carcass and took the ring, hiding it carefully. The men did not see what she took, but then no one was paying much attention.

The king asked who Bera was, because he did not recognize her. She gave whatever answer she thought best, although it was not the truth.

The king then returned home and Bera found herself swept along among his followers. The queen, now very cheerful, made Bera welcome, inquiring who she was. As before, Bera concealed the truth.

The queen prepared a great feast and had the bear meat readied for the men's enjoyment. The freeman's daughter was in the queen's chamber, unable to get away because the queen was suspicious about her identity. Sooner than expected, the queen entered the room with a plate of bear meat. She told Bera to eat, but Bera did not want to eat.

'How uncommonly rude,' said the queen, 'that you reject the hospitality that the queen herself has chosen to offer you. Eat it quickly, otherwise something worse will be prepared for you.'

The queen cut a small piece of the meat for Bera, and in the end Bera ate it. The queen then cut another piece and put it into Bera's mouth. Bera swallowed a small morsel of it, then spat the rest out of her mouth. She declared that she would not eat any more, even if she were to be tortured or killed. 'It may be,' said the queen, 'that this bit will be enough,' and she burst out laughing.

Bera then escaped and went home to her father. She had a very difficult pregnancy. She told her father the whole story relating to her condition and the reasons for what had happened. A little while later she fell ill and gave birth to a boy, though of an extraordinary kind. He was a man above the navel, but an elk below that. He was named Elk-Frodi. She bore another son, who was named Thorir. He had dog's feet from his insteps down. Because of this, he was called Thorir Hound's Foot; otherwise, he was the most handsome of men. A third boy was born, and this one was the most promising. He was named Bodvar, and there was no blemish on him.[47] Bera loved Bodvar the most.

The boys shot up like weeds. When they were at the games with other men, they were fierce and unyielding in everything. Men received rough treatment at their hands. Frodi* maimed many of the king's men, and some of them he killed. So matters continued until the boys were twelve years old. By then, because they were so strong that none of the king's men could stand up to them, they were no longer permitted to take part in the games.

Next Frodi told his mother that he wanted to leave, because 'I am not able to contest with the men. They are nothing but fools, easily injured as soon as they are touched.'

She said that his being among people did not suit him because he had an unyielding nature. His mother took him to the cave. She showed him the treasure that his father had intended for him, for Bjorn had long before determined what each son should have. Frodi, whose allotted share of the wealth was the smallest, wanted to take more but was unable to do so. Then he saw the weapons protruding from the rock. First he grasped the sword hilt, but it remained fast in the stone and he was unable to remove it. Next he seized the axe handle, but it too remained fast in the stone.

Then Elk-Frodi said, 'The one who brought these treasures here seems to have intended that the division of weapons should follow along the same lines as the division of the other property.'

He grasped the handle of the remaining weapon, a short sword that came loose at once. He looked at the sword for a while, and then said, 'The one who divided these treasures was unjust.'

Taking hold of the sword with both hands, he struck at the rock,

* Here Frodi is used as a shortened form of Elk-Frodi.

intending to smash the weapon to pieces. But the sword without breaking plunged into the stone right up to the hilt. Then Elk–Frodi said, 'No matter how I wield this nasty thing, it clearly knows how to bite.' After that he set out on his way, parting without even bidding his mother farewell. Frodi went to a road high in the mountains, where he attacked travellers, killing for money. He built himself a hut and settled in.

## 21. *Thorir Becomes King of the Gauts*

King Hring thought he now understood what magic lay behind all these events, yet he kept this to himself, behaving just as calmly as before.

A little later Thorir Hound's Foot asked permission to leave. His mother showed him the way to the cave and to the treasures that were intended for him. She spoke about the weapons, telling him to take the axe, declaring that his father had wanted him to have it. Then Thorir wished his mother farewell and left.

Thorir went first to the sword hilt, but the sword held fast. Then he grasped the axeshaft and the axe loosened, because it was intended for him. He took what was his and went on his way. He planned his journey so that he could first visit his brother Elk–Frodi. Thorir entered Elk–Frodi's hut and sat down, letting his hood slide over his face. A little later Frodi came home. He looked askance at the newly arrived man, then drew his short sword and said:

7. Growls the sword
   leaving the sheath.
   The hand remembers
   the work of battle.[48]

Driving his sword deep into the bench beside Thorir, Frodi became savage and threatening. Thorir then said:

8. I allowed
   on another wide road
   my axe to shout
   the same sound.

Now Thorir stopped concealing himself, and Frodi recognized his brother. He offered Thorir half of everything he had amassed, because he had no lack of wealth, but Thorir did not want to accept this gift. Thorir stayed with his brother for a while and then set off. Elk-Frodi showed him the path to Gautland, advising him that the king of the Gauts had just died and that Thorir should go to their kingdom.[49]

Elk-Frodi instructed Thorir, saying, 'It is the law of the Gauts that a great assembly is called and all the Gauts are summoned to go there. A large throne, big enough for two men to sit comfortably on, is placed in the midst of the assembly. Then the man who fills that seat is chosen king. It seems to me that you would amply fill that seat.'

The brothers parted with affection, each wishing the other well. Thorir continued on his way until he reached Gautland. He came to a jarl, who received him well, and there Thorir spent the night. Every man who saw Thorir said that he might well become the king of the Gauts because of his size. They predicted that there would be few like him at the assembly.

When the time for the assembly arrived, the proceedings went as Frodi, his brother, had predicted they would. A judge was appointed to decide the matter truthfully. Many sat in the seat, but the judge declared none of them fit for the honour. Waiting until last, Thorir sat quickly in the chair, and the judge said, 'The seats fits you best, and you are selected to receive the kingship.'

Then the people of the land gave him the name of king. He was called King Thorir Hound's Foot, and there are great sagas about him. He was well liked and he fought many battles, in which he was most often victorious. Thorir now stayed in his own kingdom for a time.

## 22. Bodvar's Vengeance

Bodvar remained at home with his mother, who loved him dearly. Of all men, he was the most accomplished and handsome, but as yet he had not met very many people. Once he asked his mother who his father was. She told him about his father's killing, giving her son all the information. She explained how Bjorn had fallen under the spell of his stepmother.[50]

Bodvar said, 'We have wrongs to repay this witch.'

Then Bera told him how the queen had forced her to eat the bear's flesh, 'and the result can be seen in your brothers, Thorir Hound's Foot and Elk-Frodi'.

Bodvar said, 'I think Frodi ought to have felt more bound to take vengeance on this cowardly witch for our father than to kill innocent men for their money and carry out other vile acts. Likewise, I think it is odd that Thorir went away without giving this ogress something to remember. So it seems to me that I should punish her on our behalf.'

Bera replied, 'Arrange it so that she is not able to use her black arts to injure you.'

He said that it would be so arranged.

Bera and Bodvar now went to see the king. Following Bodvar's advice, Bera explained to the king how everything had come about. She showed him the ring, which she had taken from under the shoulder of the beast, explaining that Bjorn, his son, had owned it.

The king agreed that without a doubt he recognized the ring; 'I suspected that the queen was behind the strange events that have happened here, but for the sake of my love for her I have let matters remain quiet.'

Bodvar said, 'Send her away now or else we will take vengeance on her.'

The king said that he wished to compensate Bodvar for his loss with as much treasure as he might want, but that matters were to remain quiet, as they had been before. He would give Bodvar a position of command, the title of jarl straightaway and, after his days were over, the kingdom, if only no harm were done to her.

Bodvar replied that he did not want to be king; rather he said that he wanted to be with the king and to serve him. 'You are so trapped by this monster that you hardly have the wits to run your rightful kingdom, and from now on she will never thrive in this place.'

Bodvar became so filled with fury that the king dared not stand in his way. Carrying a pouch in his hand, Bodvar went to the queen's chamber; the king and Bodvar's mother followed after him. Bodvar entered the chamber and turned to Queen Hvit. He placed the rough leather bag over her head. Then he pulled it down and tied it around her throat. He knocked her off her feet and with beatings and torments sent her to Hel, dragging her through every street.[51]

Many or most of those who were within the hall thought this punishment was only half of what she deserved. The king, however, took it very badly, but there was nothing he could do about it. In this way Queen Hvit lost her miserable life.

Bodvar was eighteen years old when this happened. A little later King Hring took sick and died. Bodvar became the ruler of the kingdom, but he was content with this position for only a short while. Then he called an assembly of the men of the land. At that meeting he announced that he wanted to leave and that he was marrying his mother to the man named Valsleyt, a jarl already in the land. Bodvar took part in the wedding feast before riding away.

## 23. Bodvar and His Brothers

After the wedding Bodvar rode away alone. He took with him neither much gold or silver, nor other valuables. Yet he was well equipped with weapons and clothes and was riding on his good horse. Following his mother's instructions, he first headed to the cave. The sword loosened as soon as he gripped the hilt. It was in this sword's nature that it could never be drawn without causing the death of a man and that it should not be laid under a man's head or rested on its hilt. Only three times in its owner's life could the weapon be urged to action. Thereafter it could never be drawn again by the same person, so difficult was its nature.[52] All the brothers wanted to own so valuable a treasure.

Bodvar set out to find his brother Elk-Frodi. He made a sheath for the sword from some birch wood. There is nothing noteworthy to tell about his journey until he arrived late in the day at a large hall. Here Elk-Frodi ruled. Bodvar led his horse into the stable, acting as though he had a right to everything that he wanted. Frodi came home in the evening; he glared at the newcomer. Bodvar did not react noticeably but remained quiet. The horses meanwhile started to go at each other, each trying to drive the other from the stall.

Frodi then said, 'Truly it is an aggressive man who dares to seat himself inside without my permission.'

Bodvar pulled the hood over his face and gave no reply. Elk-Frodi stood up. Then drawing his short sword, he struck downward, burying the weapon up to the hilt. He then did the same thing again, but Bodvar did not flinch. Raising his sword for the third time, Elk-Frodi now turned aggressively on Bodvar. It seemed to Elk-Frodi that the new-comer did not know the meaning of fear, and he intended to master him.

When Bodvar understood Frodi's intentions, he decided to wait no longer. Springing to his feet, he dashed in under the other's arms. Elk-Frodi had a powerful grip, and they found themselves locked in a hard struggle. Then Bodvar's hood fell down.

Frodi, recognizing his brother, said, 'Welcome, kinsman. We have wrestled far too long.'

'It has as yet done no damage,' said Bodvar.

Elk-Frodi replied, 'It would, however, be safer for you, kinsman, to stop fighting with me. Should we start fighting in earnest, holding nothing back, you would realize the difference in strength between us.'

Frodi invited him to remain there, offering him a half-share of everything. But Bodvar declined. He thought it wrong to kill people for their wealth, and so he prepared to leave.

Frodi accompanied Bodvar on his way. He told Bodvar that he had given quarter to many men, especially those who were small and weak. Bodvar, cheered up by his brother's remark, praised him, saying that in this he did well, 'and you should let most people go in peace, even if you find fault with them.'

Elk-Frodi answered, 'To me everything is ill-given. But for you, the choice is clear: Go to King Hrolf. All the foremost champions want to be with him. His generosity, as well as his magnificence and courage, exceeds by far all other kings.'

Then Frodi reached over and pushed Bodvar, saying, 'Kinsman, you are not as strong as you should be.' Frodi drew blood from his own calf, telling Bodvar to drink of it, and Bodvar did so.

Then Frodi shoved his brother for a second time, but Bodvar stood firm in his tracks. 'You are now exceedingly strong, kinsman,' said Frodi. 'I believe the drink has been of use to you. From now on, you will be ahead of most men in strength and prowess as well as in courage and nobility. This thought pleases me immensely.'

Next Frodi stamped on the stone that lay nearby. His leg sank into the rock up to the small nub on the back of the leg above the elk-hoof.[53] He said, 'I will come to this hoofprint every day in order to see what is in it. It will be earth if you have died of sickness; water if you have drowned; but blood if you have been killed by weapons. If it is the last, then I will avenge you, because I love you best of all men.'

With this they parted, and Bodvar went on his way. He arrived in Gautland, but King Thorir Hound's Foot was not at home. Bodvar and Thorir looked so much alike that the one could not be distinguished from the other, so people thought that Thorir had returned home. Bodvar was placed in the high seat and served in all ways as though he were the king. Since Thorir was married, Bodvar was put to bed with the queen.

But Bodvar would not get under the bed cover with her, which she thought strange because she truly believed him to be her husband. Bodvar told her everything, and she for her part kept the secret. So they continued in this way, talking together every night with a blanket separating them, until Thorir returned home. Then people realized who Bodvar was, and the brothers held a joyful reunion. Thorir said that he would have trusted no other man to lie so close to his queen.

Thorir invited Bodvar to stay with them, offering him half of all his movable property, but Bodvar said that he did not want to do that.

Thorir then suggested that Bodvar choose whatever he desired to take away with him, offering also to supply him with a troop of men. But again Bodvar refused.

Bodvar now rode out, and Thorir accompanied him for a way. The brothers parted in friendship, but also with unspoken misgivings. Nothing is said of Bodvar's travels until he arrived in Denmark and was only a short distance from Hleidargard.

One day a heavy rainstorm soaked Bodvar thoroughly. His horse, which he had ridden hard, was exhausted under him. The going was heavy since the ground had turned to mud. That night it grew very dark and the downpour continued steadily. Bodvar took no notice until his horse stumbled on a large obstacle. He dismounted and looked around, soon realizing that he had come upon some sort of house. He found the door, knocked on it and a man came out of the house. Bodvar asked for shelter for the night. The farmer answered that he would not send him away in the dead of night, especially as he was a stranger. From what the farmer could see, the stranger seemed to be very imposing. Bodvar stayed there overnight and was treated hospitably. He asked many questions about the exploits of King Hrolf and his champions, inquiring also about the distance to Hleidargard.

'It is now a very short distance,' said the farmer. 'Do you intend to go there?'

'Yes,' replied Bodvar, 'that is my intention.'

The farmer declared that it would be fitting for him to do so, 'because I see you are a large, powerful man, and they think themselves great champions'. And the old woman living there sobbed aloud, as she did whenever they mentioned King Hrolf and his champions at Hleidargard.

Bodvar asked, 'Why are you crying, you simple old woman?'

The old woman said, 'My husband and I have one son, who is named Hott. One day he went to the stronghold to amuse himself, but the king's men taunted him. He could not stand up to such conduct, so the men took hold of him and stuck him into a pile of bones. It is their habit at mealtimes, when they are finished gnawing the meat from a bone, to throw it at him. Sometimes, if the bone hits him, he is badly injured. Whether he is alive or dead I do not know. But I ask this reward from you, in return for my hospitality, that you throw smaller bones at him rather than larger ones; that is, if he is not already dead.'[54]

Bodvar answered, 'I will do as you request, but I do not think it is warriorlike to strike people with bones or to harm children or men of small account.'

'Then you will do well,' said the old woman, 'because your hand seems to be strong, and I know for certain that, if you chose not to hold back, an opponent would have no refuge from your blows.'

Bodvar continued on his way to Hleidargard. After arriving at the king's royal residence, he immediately stabled his horse in the stall with the king's best mounts without asking anyone's permission. Then he entered the hall, where there were only a few men. He sat down near the entrance, and after he had been there for a short time, he heard a noise coming from somewhere in the corner. Bodvar looked in that direction and saw a man's hand emerging from a huge pile of bones lying there. The hand was very black.

Bodvar walked over to the corner and asked who was in the bone pile. He was answered, though timidly, 'My name is Hott, kind sir.'

'Why are you here?' asked Bodvar. 'Or what are you doing?'

Hott's reply was, 'I am making myself a shield wall, kind sir.'

'You and your shield wall are pathetic,' said Bodvar. He grabbed hold of the man and yanked him out of the bone pile.

Hott screamed loudly and then said, 'You are acting as though you want me dead, since I had prepared my defences so well. Now you have broken my shield wall into pieces even though I had built it so high around me that it protected me against all your blows. No blow has reached me now for some time, yet the wall was not as complete as I had intended it to be.'

Bodvar said, 'You will no longer build your shield wall.'

Hott replied, 'Are you going to kill me now, kind sir?'

Bodvar, telling Hott to be quiet, picked him up and carried him from the hall to a nearby lake. Few paid attention to this. Bodvar washed Hott completely and then returned to the same place on the bench where he had sat previously. He led Hott there and sat him down beside himself. Hott was so scared that all his limbs and joints

BODVAR AND HIS BROTHERS

trembled, although he seemed to understand that this man wanted to help him.

Later in the evening men crowded into the hall. Hrolf's champions saw that Hott had been seated on one of the benches, and it seemed to them that the man who had undertaken to do that was indeed brave. Hott cast a fearful glance in the direction of his old acquaintances, for he had received only harm from them. Afraid for his life, he tried to get back to his bone pile, but Bodvar held on to Hott and he was unable to get away. Hott thought that, if he could manage to get to the heap of bones, he would not be so exposed to the men's blows.

The king's men now took up their old habits. At first they threw small bones across the floor at Bodvar and Hott. Bodvar acted as if he saw nothing. Hott was so frightened that he took neither food nor drink, expecting to be struck at any moment.

Then Hott said to Bodvar, 'Kind sir, here comes a large knuckle bone, which is intended to do us much harm.'

Bodvar told Hott to be quiet. He cupped his hand and caught the knuckle bone, which included the attached leg bone. Bodvar threw the knuckle back, and it smashed with such force into the man who had thrown it that he was killed.[55] The king's men were struck with fear.

King Hrolf and his champions up in the fortress were now told that an imposing man had arrived in the hall and had killed one of the king's retainers. The other retainers wanted to have the man put to death.

The king asked whether his follower had been killed without cause. 'Almost,' they said.

Then the full truth came out. King Hrolf said that by no means should this man be killed: 'It is a bad habit that you have adopted, throwing bones at innocent men. It brings dishonour to me and shame to you. I have repeatedly spoken to you about this matter, but you have paid no attention. I suspect that this man, whom you have now attacked, is no weakling. Summon him to me, so that I can find out who he is.'

Bodvar went before the king and greeted him artfully. The king asked for his name.

'Your retainers call me Hott's protector, but my name is Bodvar.'

The king said, 'What compensation are you prepared to offer me for my man?'

Bodvar replied, 'He got what he deserved.'

The king said, 'Do you want to be my man and occupy his place?'

Bodvar answered, 'I will not refuse to become your man, but Hott and I will not, as matters stand, be separated. We will both sit closer to you on the benches than that man did, or else we both leave.'

The king said, 'I see no honour in him, but I will not begrudge him food.'

Bodvar now chose a seat that pleased him, not bothering to sit in the place the other man had occupied. At one point he pulled three men up out of their seats, and then he and Hott sat down in their places. They had now moved much farther into the hall than earlier. Men thought Bodvar difficult to deal with, and there was strong resentment against him.

As Yuletime drew near, gloom settled over the men. Bodvar asked Hott what caused their dejection. Hott told him that a huge, monstrous beast had come there the past two winters. 'The creature has wings on its back and it usually flies. For two autumns now it has come here, causing much damage. No weapon can bite into it,[56] and the king's champions, even the greatest among them, do not return home.'[57]

Bodvar said, 'The hall is not so well manned as I had thought, if one animal alone could destroy the king's lands and his livestock.'

Hott said, 'It is not an animal, rather it is the greatest of trolls.'[58]

Then came Yule eve, and the king said, 'It is my wish that tonight men remain calm, making no noise, and I forbid any of my men to put themselves in danger with the beast. The livestock will be left to their fate, because I do not want to lose any of my men.' Everyone faithfully promised the king to do as he asked.

Bodvar stole away in the night and took Hott with him. Hott went only after being forced to do so, declaring that he was being steered straight toward death. Bodvar said, 'Things will turn out for the better.'

They now left the hall behind them, with Bodvar carrying Hott because he was so frightened. They saw the creature, and immediately Hott started to scream as loudly as he could, crying that the beast would swallow him. Bodvar told the dog to be quiet and threw him down on the moor. There he lay, not a little scared, at the same time not daring to go home.

Bodvar now went against the beast. He was hampered by his sword, which, as he tried to draw it, stuck fast in its scabbard. Determined, Bodvar urged the sword out until the scabbard squeaked. Then he grasped the scabbard and the sword came out of the sheath. Immediately he thrust it up under the beast's shoulder, striking so hard that the blade reached quickly into the heart. Then the beast fell dead to the ground.

After this encounter Bodvar went to the place where Hott was lying. He picked up Hott and carried him to where the beast lay dead. Hott was trembling violently.

Bodvar said, 'Now you will drink the beast's blood.' For a while Hott was unwilling, although certainly he dared do nothing else. Bodvar made him drink two large mouthfuls as well as eat some of the beast's heart.[59] After that Bodvar seized Hott, and they fought each other for a long time.

Bodvar said, 'You have now become remarkably strong, and I expect that from this day forward you will have no fear of King Hrolf's retainers.'

Hott replied, 'From now on, I will fear neither them nor you.'

'Then, Hott, my friend,' said Bodvar, 'things have turned out well. Let us now go back to the beast, raising him up in such a way that men will think the creature must be alive.'

They did just that and afterward went home. They kept these events to themselves, and so no one knew what they had done.

In the morning, the king asked what was known about the beast, whether it had visited them in the night. He was told that all the livestock were safe in the pens, unharmed. The king ordered men to inquire if there were any indications that the beast had visited them. The guards went out but quickly returned. They told the king that the beast was coming toward them, furiously advancing on the stronghold. The king ordered his retainers to be valiant. Each was to do his best according to his courage, so that they might overcome this monster. Obeying the king's command, the men prepared themselves.

The king looked toward the beast, saying finally, 'I see no movement in it, but which one of you will now seize the opportunity to go against it?'

Bodvar said, 'That would likely satisfy the curiosity of the bravest man. Hott, my friend, throw off the slander that men have laid on you, claiming that you have neither spirit nor courage. Go and kill the beast. You can see that no one else is too eager to do so.'

'Right,' said Hott, 'I will set myself to that task.'

The king said, 'I do not know where your courage has come from, Hott, but much has changed about you in a short time.'

Hott said, 'For this task, give me the sword Golden Hilt, the one that you are holding, and then I will either kill the beast or find my own death.'[60]

King Hrolf said, 'That sword is not to be carried except by a man who is both strong in body and noble in spirit.'

Hott replied, 'Assume, Sire, that I am made from such a mould.'

The king retorted, 'How can one tell? Perhaps more has changed about you than is evident. Few would think that you are the same person. Take the sword, for it will serve you well if my instincts about you turn out to be correct.'

Then Hott went boldly against the beast, thrusting at it as soon as he was within striking distance. The beast fell down dead.

Bodvar said, 'See, Sire, what he has now accomplished.'

The king answered, 'Certainly he has changed greatly, but Hott alone did not kill the beast; rather you did it.'

Bodvar said, 'That may be.'

The king said, 'I knew when you came here that few would be your equal, but it seems to me that your finest achievement is that you have made Hott into another champion. He was previously thought to be a man in whom there was little probability of much luck. I do not want him called Hott any longer; instead, from now on he will be called Hjalti.[61] You will now be called after the sword Golden Hilt.'

And here ends this tale of Bodvar and his brothers.

## 24. King Hrolf's Champions

Now the winter passed until the time when the king's berserkers were expected home. Bodvar asked Hjalti about the berserkers' habits, and Hjalti replied that, 'Upon returning to the king's guard, it was their custom to challenge each and every man. They begin with the king, asking him if he considers himself their equal. The king answers, "That is difficult to say with men who are as valiant as you are. You have distinguished yourselves in battles and bloodlettings with many peoples in the southern regions of the world as well as here in the North." The king answers in this way, more from courage than from fear, because he knows their minds, and they have won great victories for him. Next they ask every man in the hall the same question, but no one reckons himself their equal.'

Bodvar replied, 'King Hrolf's choice of warriors is limited if everyone turns cowardly because of the berserkers.' After this remark, they stopped talking.

Bodvar had now been with King Hrolf a year when the second Yule arrived. As the king sat at the table, all at once the doors of the hall burst open and twelve berserkers rushed into the hall. With all the iron in their equipment, they were as grey as broken ice. Bodvar quietly asked Hjalti if he dared to pit himself against one of them.

'Yes,' answered Hjalti, 'not against one, but rather against all. I now have no fear even when I face overwhelming odds, and one of them alone does not set me to trembling.'

The berserkers, advancing into the hall, saw that the number of King Hrolf's champions had increased since their departure. They studied the newcomers carefully, noting that one especially was no weakling. It is said that they were a little taken aback by what they found in front of them. The berserkers went, as was their custom, before King Hrolf. They questioned him, as usual, with the same words. The king answered them, as usual, in words that seemed best to him, offering his usual reply. Then they went up to each man in the hall, coming at last to the two companions. The leader of the berserkers asked Bodvar whether he considered himself an equal.

Bodvar answered that he did not regard himself as equally able, but rather as abler. He added that this difference would be found in whatever way that they might test themselves, and that the berserker – a stinking son of a mare – ought not to come sidling up to him like a common sow. Bodvar lunged at the berserker, seizing him and then heaving him up in the air in his full armour. He then threw the berserker to the ground with such force that the man lay there as if his bones had been broken.

Elsewhere in the hall, Hjalti played much the same game.

Now there was a great disturbance in the hall, and the king, sensing the danger of the situation, realized that his men might start to fight among themselves. Quickly leaving his high seat, he approached Bodvar, asking him to help calm the men and return the hall to good order. But Bodvar said that the berserker would lose his life unless he declared himself the lesser man. King Hrolf said that this could easily be accomplished, and Bodvar let the man stand up. Hjalti did the same, in accordance with the king's command. The men now returned to their seats. The berserkers, too, took their places, although they had much on their minds.

King Hrolf began a persuasive speech. He explained to them that they could now see that nothing existed so famous, so strong, or so big that an equal could not be found. 'I forbid you to awaken any animosity in my hall. If you defy me in this matter, you will pay with your lives. Be as savage as you like when I have dealings with my enemies and thus win honour and renown. Now, however, I have so choice a selection of champions that I do not need to depend upon you beserkers.'

The king's speech was well received, and the men were fully reconciled with one another.

The hall was now arranged in the following manner: Bodvar, who had become the most esteemed and the highest valued, sat at the king's right. Then came Hjalti the Magnanimous; it was the king himself who gave him that name. Hjalti was called the Magnanimous for this reason: he spent every day with the king's retainers, the same ones who had treated him so badly, as has been told earlier, yet Hjalti did them no injury, although he had now become a man far greater than they. The king would have thought it excusable had Hjalti given them some reminder, even killing one or another of them. On the king's left hand sat the three brothers – Svipdag, Hvitserk and Beygad – so important had they become. Next came the twelve berserkers. All the other heroes were then seated on both sides the length of the stronghold, but they are not named here.

The king arranged that his men take part in all kinds of sports and refinements, as well as amusements and pleasures of every kind. In whatever contests were tried, Bodvar proved the foremost of all the king's champions. He came to be held in so much esteem by King Hrolf that the king gave to him in marriage Drifa, his only daughter.[62] And so time passed for a while. They sat at home in the kingdom and were the most famous of men.

## 25. Bodvar Encourages King Hrolf to Recover His Inheritance

It is said that one day King Hrolf sat in his royal hall. He was holding a costly feast in company with all his champions and his great men and, as the king looked to both sides, he said, 'Overwhelming strength has been assembled here in this hall.'

Next King Hrolf asked Bodvar whether he knew of any king his equal, or of one who commanded such champions. Bodvar replied that he did not, but added 'to my mind there is one thing that diminishes your royal status'.

King Hrolf asked what that might be. Bodvar said, 'It is a shortcoming, Sire, that you have not yet recovered from Uppsala your father's inheritance, the one that King Adils, your in-law, unjustly withholds.'[63]

King Hrolf said it would be difficult to seek that wealth, 'because King Adils is not a simple man. Rather, he is skilled in the black arts; a crafty, guileful, cunning and cruel-hearted man who is the worst to contend against.'

Bodvar said, 'Nevertheless, it would be fitting for you, Sire, to seek your allotted share, meeting once with King Adils in order to learn how he would answer such a claim.'

King Hrolf replied, 'It is a grave action that you are proposing. Wherever King Adils, the ambitious and the guileful is, we have a debt of vengeance for my father. All the same, we will risk it.'

Bodvar said, 'Just this once I would like to find out what King Adils is made of.'[64]

## 26. *Three Strange Nights with Hrani*

King Hrolf prepared himself for his journey, assembling a hundred men in addition to his twelve champions and his twelve berserkers. Nothing is told of their travels until they came upon a farmer, who was standing outside as they rode up. He invited all the king's men to stay at his house. The king answered, 'You are a bold man, but do you have the means for this? We are not so few, and more than a small farmer is needed to take care of all of us.'

The farmer laughed, saying, 'Yes, Sire, I have at times seen no fewer men come to where I have been. You will lack neither drink nor anything else that you might need during the night.'

The king said, 'Then we will risk it.' The farmer was pleased with this decision. The newcomers' horses were taken care of and shown proper treatment.

'What is your name, farmer?' asked the king.

'Some men call me Hrani,' he answered.[65]

The hospitality was so good at Hrani's that the king felt he had rarely been received with so much generosity. The farmer was full of cheer, and there was no question to which he did not have an answer. They found him to be no fool.

They now went to sleep, but they awoke to such extreme cold that their teeth were chattering. They all got up together, dressed and covered themselves with whatever they could find. All, that is, except for the king's champions, who were content with the clothing they already were wearing. Everyone felt the cold throughout the night.

The farmer asked, 'How have you slept?'

'Well,' replied Bodvar.

Then the farmer spoke to the king, 'I know that your retainers found it cold in the hall during the night, and so it was. They cannot be expected to withstand the hardships that King Adils will try on you in Uppsala, if they thought this trial was so difficult. Send home half your company, Sire, if you want to stay alive, because it is not with a large force that you will overcome King Adils.'

'You are an impressive man, farmer,' said the king. 'And I will adopt the counsel that you offer.'

When they had prepared themselves they set out, wishing the farmer well. The king sent home half his force. The rest rode on their way, and at once another small farm appeared in their path. They thought they recognized the same farmer with whom they had just stayed. Matters now seemed to them to be taking a strange turn.

The farmer greeted them well, asking why they came so often. The king replied, 'We hardly know what tricks we are facing. You might be called a truly crafty fellow.'

The farmer said, 'Again you will not be poorly received.'

They were there another night and were shown fine hospitality. They fell asleep but were awakened by a thirst they found almost unbearable. They could hardly move their tongues in their mouths, so they got up and went to a vat filled with wine and drank from it.

In the morning farmer Hrani spoke, 'Once again, Sire, matters are such that you might well listen to me. I think that there is little endurance in the men who drank during the night. You will have to endure trials more difficult than that when you visit King Adils.'

Suddenly a fierce storm struck, so the men remained there that day and the third night came. Again a fire was built for them in the evening, and those who sat near the fire felt the heat on their hands. Most of the men quickly abandoned the places on the benches that farmer Hrani had allotted them, with everyone moving back from the flame except King Hrolf and his champions.

The farmer said, 'Yet again Sire, you can cull from your company, and it is my counsel that no one should go except you and your twelve champions. Then there would be some hope that you will return, but otherwise there is none.'

King Hrolf replied, 'You impress me, farmer, as so sensible that we will take your advice.' They stayed there three nights.

The king rode out with twelve men, sending back the rest of his company. King Adils learned of Hrolf's progress and said that it was well that King Hrolf had chosen to visit him, 'because, before we part, he will surely have an errand here, and the stories about it will be thought well worth the telling.'

## 27. King Adils' Deceitful Welcome

King Hrolf and his champions rode up to King Adils' hall. All the townsfolk crowded into the highest towers of the stronghold to see the splendour of King Hrolf and his champions, they were equipped so handsomely. Many of the townsfolk admired such chivalrous knights.[66] At first the men rode slowly and grandly, but when they were a short distance from the hall they let the horses feel the spurs. They raced onward to the hall and all in their path, both man and beast, leapt out of the way.

King Adils had his men receive the arrivals with graciousness and ordered that their horses be attended to. Bodvar said, 'Pay attention, boys, not to tangle either the forelock or the tail. Tend them well, watching carefully that they do not soil themselves.'

King Adils was told immediately of the care they showed concerning the stabling of their horses. He said, 'Their insolence and arrogance are vast. Follow my counsel and do as I order. Cut off the tails of the horses up to the rump, and cut the forelocks in such a way that the skin on the forehead peels off. Treat them in all ways with as much ridicule as you can. Just leave them barely alive.'

Then the newcomers were led to the doors of the hall, but King Adils was nowhere in sight. 'I am,' said Svipdag, 'familiar with this place from before. I will go in first, because I am suspicious about what the manner of our reception will be and what is in store for us. We must give no indication as to which of us is King Hrolf, making King Adils unable to recognize him in our company.'

Then Svipdag placed himself in front of the group, followed by his brothers, Hvitserk and Beygad. Next came King Hrolf and Bodvar, and then all the champions one after the other. There was no one to take their measure, because Adils' men, who had escorted them to the hall, had disappeared. Hrolf's company had their hawks on their shoulders, which at that time was considered a display of gallantry. King Hrolf's hawk was called Habrok.

Svipdag led the way. He carefully examined everything, noting the many changes that had been made. Hrolf's company made its way past so many obstacles set in its path that it is not easy to record them all. The further the men went into the hall, the more difficult the going became. This continued all the way until they saw where King Adils, bloated with pride, sat on his high seat. When the one side saw the other, each realized that an important moment had come. Hrolf's company understood that it still would be difficult to reach King Adils, even though they had come so close that they were within speaking distance.

Then King Adils began to speak, 'So, Svipdag my friend, you have now come. What might be the errand of the champion here? Or are these matters not as they appear to be:

9. A dent is in the back of his skull,
   the eye is out of the head,
   a scar is in the forehead,
   two blows on the hand.

Also his brother Beygad is all crippled.'

Svipdag now spoke in so loud a voice that all could hear: 'I ask at this time to receive from you, King Adils, safe-conduct for these twelve men who have come here. I make this request in accordance with the agreement that I earlier made with you.'

King Adils replied, 'I will agree to this. With a secure feeling go now quickly and bravely into the hall.'

Within the hall they expected to find pits, dug as traps, but it proved difficult to ascertain what had been prepared to thwart them. It was so dim around King Adils that they could scarcely see his face. They could see that the ornamental wall hangings, which ringed the hall, had been broken from their mountings and moved forward, seeming to provide cover for armed men lying in wait. This assumption turned out to be correct, because a man in mail coat pushed forward from under each fold as King Hrolf and his champions made their way past the pits. King Hrolf and his champions found themselves engaged in a hard fight, and they cleaved their opponents as far down as their teeth. King Adils' men were piled in heaps, and still they were unable to determine which one was King Hrolf.

In his high seat, King Adils swelled with rage when he saw Hrolf's champions cutting down his troops like dogs. Realizing that the game could not go on in this way, he stood up and said, 'What is the meaning of this fighting? You are acting like scoundrels, attacking men of distinction who have visited us. Stop immediately and seat yourselves. Kinsman Hrolf, let us all set about greeting one other with good cheer.'

Svipdag said, 'You show little regard for the truce, King Adils, and you will find no renown in such conduct.' After that they sat down. Svipdag sat closest to the wall, next to Hjalti the Magnanimous, followed by Bodvar, who sat beside the king. They still wanted King Hrolf to remain unrecognized.

King Adils said, 'I see that you do not travel in a foreign land in a dignified manner, or why, kinsman Hrolf, do you not travel with a larger following?'

Svipdag replied, 'I see that you do not shrink from working treacherously against King Hrolf and his men; it is not your concern whether he rides here with few or with many men.'

And so they ended their talk.

## 28. King Adils Attempts to Defeat King Hrolf

King Adils ordered the hall cleaned, and the dead were carried out. Many of his men had been killed and a large number were wounded.

King Adils said, 'Let us make fires the length of the hall for our friends and show genuine hospitality to these worldly guests so that everyone will be pleased.'

Men were then sent to light the fire. Meanwhile, King Hrolf and his men sat with their weapons, never letting them out of their reach. The flames increased quickly, as neither pitch nor dry wood was spared. King Adils and his retainers arranged themselves on one side of the fire, and King Hrolf and his champions were on the other side. Each group sat on a long bench, and they spoke graciously across to each other.

King Adils said, 'Concerning you, champions of King Hrolf, there is no exaggeration in what is said about your valour. Of course, you think yourselves better than anyone else, but there is no lie in what is said about your stamina. Now build up the fires,' said King Adils, 'because I cannot discern clearly which one of you is the king. They will not flee from the fire, even if they are rather warmed by it.'

So it was done as Adils instructed. He wanted in this way to learn for certain where King Hrolf was, assuming that Hrolf would not be able to tolerate the heat as well as his champions. To Adils it seemed that it would be easier to get hold of Hrolf, when he knew for certain where he was. Truly King Adils wanted King Hrolf dead.

Bodvar realized this fact, as did several of the others, and they could only shelter the king partly from the heat. They did this as well as they could, but not so much that he would be revealed. As the fire burned at its fiercest, King Hrolf concentrated on reminding himself that he had sworn to flee neither fire nor iron. He realized that King Adils intended to make this situation a trial: he and his champions would either burn there or fail to fulfil their solemn vow. Now they saw that King Adils had moved his throne all the way back to the outer wall of the hall, as his men also did.

More fuel was constantly being piled on the fire. King Hrolf and his men saw that the fire would reach them unless something was done. Their clothes had already been scorched when they threw their shields into the fire. Together Bodvar and Svipdag said:

10. Let's feed the fires
    In Adils' stronghold

Next, each of them seized one of the men who were feeding the flames. Bodvar and Svipdag each pitched his man into the fire and said, 'Enjoy the fire's warmth in return for your pains and labour, because we are completely baked. Now it is your turn to bake because of your diligence in building a fire for us.'

Hjalti at his end seized a third man and threw him into the flames; then they did the same to all the men who kept working the fires. Nobody was saved, and they all burned to ashes because no one dared to approach the fire.

Then, King Hrolf said:

11. He flees no fire
    who jumps over it.

Next Hrolf and all his champions, intending to seize Adils, jumped over the fire. When King Adils saw what they were doing, he saved himself by running to the tree that stood in the hall. The tree was hollow, and so he used his magic and sorcery to escape from the hall.

Next King Adils entered Queen Yrsa's room, intending to speak with her. She received him coldly and said many harsh things to him, 'You first had my husband King Helgi killed and you behaved deceitfully toward him, keeping his property from its rightful owner. And now you wish to kill my son. You are the cruellest and the most terrible of men. I will make every effort to see that King Hrolf gets the property and that you suffer a fitting disgrace.'

King Adils answered: 'Matters are such that neither of us here will trust the other. From now on, I will not come into your sight.' With this their talk ended.

Queen Yrsa went to meet King Hrolf and greeted him heartily. He welcomed her greeting. She arranged for a man to serve Hrolf and provided gracious hospitality to his company. When the servingman came before King Hrolf, he said, 'This man's face is thin and angular like a ladder carved from a pole* – and this man is your king?'[67]

King Hrolf said, 'You have given me the name kraki and it will stick to me; but what gift will you give me to confirm the name-fastening?'

The man, who was named Vogg, answered, 'I have nothing to give, because I am a man without property.'

* A kraki.

King Hrolf said, 'He who has must give.' He pulled a gold ring off his own arm and gave it to the man.

Vogg said, 'Of all the men who give, you are the most fortunate, and that is the best of treasures.'

But the king found that Vogg attached too much value to the gift and said, 'Vogg rejoices in little.'

Vogg, putting one foot up on the bench, said, 'I swear this oath: I will avenge you, if I live longer and if you are killed by men.'

The king said, 'You mean well, though there are others more likely to undertake this project than you.'

They understood that this man would be faithful and true in the small ways in which he could contribute. They thought, however, that Vogg was destined only for minor accomplishments because he was a man of little account. From then on they concealed nothing from him. Now they wanted to sleep, and they believed that they could rest without fear in the rooms chosen for them by the queen.

Bodvar said, 'Things have been nicely prepared for us here and the queen wishes us well, but King Adils wishes us as much harm as he can cause. I would be greatly surprised if events conclude as they are now.'

Vogg told them that King Adils was so devoted a heathen sacrificer 'that his like can not be found. He sacrifices to a boar, and I scarcely understand that such a monster can exist. Be on your guard, because King Adils is putting all his energy into looking for a way to destroy you.'

'I think the possibility more likely,' said Bodvar, 'that he will remember having to leave the hall this evening because of us.'

'You should keep in mind,' said Vogg, 'that he will prove to be cunning and savage.'

After this conversation they fell asleep, but a noise from outside awoke them. The noise was so loud that it echoed everywhere, and the house in which they were sleeping shook and swayed as if it was on soft ground. Vogg began to speak, 'Now the boar has been set in motion, sent by King Adils to take revenge on you. It is such a great troll that no one can stand against it.'

King Hrolf had with him a great hound named Gram;[68] it was outstandingly brave and strong. The troll burst into the house. It had the likeness of a boar,[69] and hideous sounds came from its trollish nature. Bodvar set the hound against the boar, and the dog attacked without hesitation. A fierce struggle followed. Bodvar aided the hound, hewing at the boar, but his sword would not cut into the beast's back. The hound Gram was so strong that it was able to tear the ears off the boar, taking with them all the flesh from the cheeks. All at once the boar withdrew, disappearing downward from the place where it had been standing.

Next King Adils arrived outside the house with a large following of armed men. They immediately set fire to the house and, inside, King Hrolf and his champions realized that yet again there would be no shortage of fuel.

Bodvar said, 'A sad death's day if we are to be burned inside here. I would rather choose to fall before weapons on a level plain. If this burning is allowed to happen, it will be an unfortunate ending for King Hrolf's champions. I see no better plan than to hurl ourselves against the planks of the wall and in this way manage to break out of the house – if only that is possible.'

This task proved to be difficult, for the house was strongly built. 'Each one of us,' said Bodvar, 'will have his man before him when we come out, but, as previously, they will quickly lose courage.'

'It is an excellent plan,' said King Hrolf, 'and it will serve us well.'

## 29. Queen Yrsa Gives King Hrolf
### His Inheritance and More

Hrolf and his champions put the plan to work, throwing themselves against the wallboards with such force and determination that the wall broke apart and the men escaped. The area outside the hall within the fortress was packed with men in coats of mail, and a brutal battle began. King Hrolf and his champions pushed fiercely forward, thinning the ranks of King Adils' men. Faced with the strength of the champions' blows, none of King Adils' men proved to be an opponent so proud or so stubborn that he did not crumble. In the midst of the hard fighting, King Hrolf's hawk came flying out of the fortress. It settled on the king's shoulder, and from there, filled with pride, it acted as though assisting in a glorious victory.

Bodvar said, 'The hawk is behaving as if it has performed a great feat.' Adils' man, whose task it was to watch over the hawks raced up to the loft where they were kept. He thought it strange that King Hrolf's hawk had managed to get free, but then he found all of King Adils' hawks had been killed.

The battle ended with Hrolf and his men killing many of the enemy; nothing could stand against them. King Adils had disappeared, and no one had any idea what had become of him. Those of King Adils' men who were still standing asked for mercy, and it was granted.

Afterwards Hrolf's company went to King Adils' hall. Entering boldly, Bodvar asked King Hrolf on which bench he wanted to sit. King Hrolf answered, 'We will seat ourselves on the king's dais itself, and I will sit in the high seat.'

King Adils did not return to the hall. He felt that he had suffered grievously, having achieved little despite all his schemes. Hrolf and his men sat for a while in peace and quiet.

Then Hjalti the Magnanimous said, 'Would it not be wise for someone to go to the stables to check our horses to see if they require attention?' A man was sent off, but soon he returned, reporting that the horses had been shamefully abused. As recounted earlier, they had been maimed. King Hrolf showed little response beyond saying that in dealings with King Adils everything went one way.

Now Queen Yrsa came into the hall and went before King Hrolf, greeting him in a refined and elegant manner. He received her greeting well. She said, 'You have not been welcomed, kinsman, as you should have been, or as I wanted you to be. Nor ought you, my son, to remain here any longer in so inhospitable a place, because right now large numbers of troops are assembling throughout the land of the Swedes. King Adils intends to kill all of you. He has wanted to do so for a long time, had he only been able; but at this very moment your good luck has more power than his sorcery. Here is a silver horn, which I give to you. In it are kept all of King Adils' best rings, including the one called

Sviagris, the one he values most of all.'[70] So, too, she gave him a huge store of gold as well as of silver. The treasure was so large that one person could hardly conceive of its value.

Vogg was present and for his faithful service received a reward in gold from King Hrolf. The queen had twelve horses brought forward. All were reddish in colour except one, which was as white as snow and was for King Hrolf to ride. These horses were the ones that had proven themselves to be the best of King Adils' mounts; all were equipped with full armour. The queen also supplied Hrolf and his men with shields, helmets, war equipment and the best clothes that could be found, because the fire had ruined their weapons and their clothes. With generosity, she gave them everything they needed.

King Hrolf said, 'Have you given me all the property which is mine by rights and which my father owned?'

She replied, 'In many ways, it is more than I was entitled to give you, but you and your men have here won much fame. Prepare yourselves now as best you can so that you are not vulnerable, because you will be tested again.'

After that they mounted their horses. King Hrolf spoke affectionately to his mother, and they parted with tenderness.

## 30. *King Adils Is Conquered by Gold and King Hrolf Angers Hrani*

King Hrolf and his champions rode down from Uppsala, passing through the region called the Fyris Plains. The king saw a gold ring glowing on the road in front of him; it rattled with a loud sound as they rode over it. 'It bellows so loudly,' said King Hrolf, 'because it dislikes being alone.'

He slid off one of his own gold rings and tossed it to the one on the road, saying, 'It shall not happen that I stoop for gold, even if it is lying on the road. Let none of my men be so rash as to pick it up, for it has been cast here in order to delay our journey.'

They promised him that they would not touch the ring. Then, from all directions, they heard the sound of war trumpets and saw a huge force coming after them. The pursuing army was rushing forward furiously, each man forcing his horse to its fullest. King Hrolf and his champions, however, continued riding at the same pace.

Bodvar said, 'These men pursue us hard. I, for one, certainly want some of them to reach their goal, and they themselves are surely eager to find us.'

The king said, 'Take little notice. They will delay themselves.'

Then Hrolf reached out to Beygad, who rode next to him, holding in his hand the horn with the gold. The king took the horn from Beygad and threw the gold all over the road. He rode the length of the Fyris Plains sowing gold so that in the end the paths gleamed like gold. When the pursuers saw the gold glistening on the road, most of them jumped off their horses. A contest started and the best at the game was the one quickest to pick up the gold. They grabbed and brawled, and in the end, the strongest won.

The pursuit was slowed and, when King Adils realized the change in pace, he came close to losing his reason. He rebuked his men with hard words, telling them that they picked up the lesser items while letting the more valuable prize slip away. 'The foul shame will be heard in every land that we were unable to stop twelve men from escaping, despite a force as large as the one I have here pulled together from all districts of the Swedish kingdom.'[71]

Enraged, King Adils raced ahead of everyone, with a large crowd of his men following him. When Hrolf saw Adils galloping up to him, he took the ring Sviagris and threw it down on the road. When he saw the ring, King Adils said, 'The one who gave King Hrolf this treasure has been more faithful to him than to me. Nonetheless, it is I who will now enjoy it and not King Hrolf.' Adils, wanting above all else to retrieve it, reached out with the shaft of his spear to the spot where the ring lay. He bent down over his horse and guided his spear through the hole of the ring.

Seeing what Adils was doing, Hrolf turned his horse around and said, 'I have made the greatest of the Swedes stoop like a swine.' Then, just as King Adils was pulling the spear shaft with the ring on it back toward him, King Hrolf galloped up and sliced off both his buttocks right down to the bone. He did this with the sword Skofnung, the best sword ever carried in the northern lands.

King Hrolf then told King Adils to endure this shame for a time. 'Now you know where Hrolf Kraki is, the one whom you have sought for so long.'

King Adils, suffering a great loss of blood, grew faint. He was forced to turn back, all the worse for the encounter. Meanwhile, King Hrolf recovered the ring Sviagris. There the two kings parted, and it is not told whether they ever met again. Meanwhile, Hrolf's company killed all of King Adils' men who, exposing themselves to the most danger, had ridden out in front. These warriors did not need to wait long for King Hrolf and his champions, since none of the champions thought himself too good not to offer them their services. Among the champions, no one squabbled over who should act once the opportunity arose.

King Hrolf and his men now went on their way. They rode almost the whole day and, as night fell, they found a farm. The farmer came to the door, and who was it but farmer Hrani. He offered them full hospitality, declaring that their journey had not turned out much differently from what he had predicted. The king confirmed this remark, adding that Hrani was a man not blinded by the smoke of deception.

'Here, I want to give you these weapons,' said the farmer.

The king replied, 'These are hideous weapons, farmer.' There was a shield, a sword and a coat of mail, but King Hrolf refused to accept the equipment. Hrani's mood quickly changed. He nearly lost his temper, thinking that he had been shown dishonour.

Hrani said, 'You, King Hrolf, are not acting as cleverly as you think, and you are not always as wise as you might assume.' The farmer was much offended.

Now there was no staying the night and, even though it was dark outside, they prepared to ride away. Hrani's face showed only displeasure; he thought himself poorly valued. The king had refused to accept his gifts, and he did nothing to hinder their leaving if that would please them. King Hrolf and his company rode out and, as matters stood, there were no farewells.

When they had not gone very far, Bodvar halted and said, 'Good sense comes late to fools, and so it comes to me now. I suspect that we have not behaved very wisely in rejecting what we should have accepted. We may have denied ourselves victory.'

King Hrolf answered, 'I suspect the same, because that must have been Odin the Old. Certainly the man had but one eye.'

'We should turn back as quickly as we can,' said Svipdag, 'and test the truth in this matter.'

They retraced their path, but by then the farm and the man had disappeared. 'It is of no use to look for him,' said King Hrolf, 'because that man was an evil spirit.'[72]

Then they went on their way, and nothing is told of their journey until they returned to their kingdom in Denmark. There they settled in quietly. Bodvar advised the king that he should take little part in battles from then on. To Bodvar it seemed likely that they would not be attacked if they remained quiet. He said that he was fearful that the king might not be victorious from then on, if he trusted his luck in battle.

King Hrolf answered, 'Fate rules each man's life and not that foul spirit.'

Bodvar replied, 'If it were up to us, we would choose least of all to part with you. I suspect, however, that it is but a short time before momentous events affect us all.' With this they ceased their talk.

From this journey, they gained much renown.

## 31. Queen Skuld Incites King Hjorvard

A long time passed during which King Hrolf and his champions stayed peacefully in Denmark, and no one attacked them. All Hrolf's subject kings remained obedient. They paid him their tribute, as did Hjorvard, his brother-in-law.

It happened that Queen Skuld spoke with her husband King Hjorvard. Sighing heavily, she said, 'It suits me little that we should pay tribute to King Hrolf and be forced to be his underlings. You must not remain his subject.'

Hjorvard answered, 'It suits us best to suffer this indignity, as the others do, and to let everything remain quiet.'

'What a weakling you are,' she said, 'to accept whatever shame is handed to you.'

He replied, 'It is not possible to challenge King Hrolf, and no one dares raise a shield against him.'

'In this respect you are all so cowardly,' she said. 'There is no spirit in any of you, and so it will remain for those who take no risks. How will we know whether King Hrolf and his champions can be hurt unless they are put to the test? The times are changing,' she said, 'and I believe King Hrolf is a man without hope of victory. To my mind it does not seem outlandish to test if this assumption is true. Even if he is my kinsman, I will not spare him. He himself suspects that he will not gain the victory, and it is for this reason that he remains continually at home. I will now prepare a plan – one that might work – and I will spare no trouble in finding the proper way to force a showdown between us.'

Skuld was a powerful sorceress. She came from elfin stock on her mother's side, and for this fact King Hrolf and his champions would pay.

'First, I will send men to King Hrolf, asking him to relieve me of the paying of tribute for the next three years. Instead I will offer to pay him everything at once, according to his rights. I think this ruse will work, and if he accepts the idea, we need do nothing further.'

Messengers now went between them, doing as the queen wished. When asked, King Hrolf agreed to the request concerning the tribute. Time passed.

## 32. Queen Skuld Attacks King Hrolf at Yule

Meanwhile Skuld assembled a troop of the best fighters as well as the worst rabble from neighbouring provinces. This treachery was concealed so that King Hrolf was completely unaware of it. Likewise the champions suspected nothing, because it was done with the most skilful magic and sorcery. Skuld, to overpower her brother King Hrolf, fashioned a spell of high potency, which summoned elves, norns and countless other vile creatures.[73] No human power could withstand so strong a force.

Meanwhile, King Hrolf and his champions were happily revelling and amusing themselves in Hleidargard. With skill and courtesy they took part in all the games known to such men. Each of them had a mistress for his pleasure.

And now there is more to be told. When Hjorvard's and Skuld's forces were fully prepared, they set out for Hleidargard, arriving in uncountable numbers just at Yule. King Hrolf had commanded lavish preparations for the feast, and his men sat drinking deeply that Yule evening. Outside the stronghold, Hjorvard and Skuld pitched their tents, which were large and long and strangely outfitted. There were many wagons, all filled with weapons and armour. King Hrolf paid no attention to the new arrivals. His thoughts were more on his generosity, magnificence and courage. He dwelt on the valour that lay in his heart, pondering how to provide for all his guests in a way that would allow his fame to travel farthest. He already had everything that might enhance the honour of a worldly king.[74]

It is not mentioned that King Hrolf and his champions worshipped the old gods at any time. Rather, they put their trust in their own might and main.[75] The holy faith, at that time, had not been proclaimed here in the northern lands and, for this reason, those who lived in the north had little knowledge of their Creator.

Next there is this to tell, Hjalti the Magnanimous went to the house of his mistress. It was then that he saw clearly that peace was not being prepared in the tents of Hjorvard and Skuld. But Hjalti raised no alarm, and his expression showed no concern. He lay now with his mistress; she was the fairest of women. After he had been there for a while, he sprang to his feet and said, 'Which do you think better, two twenty-two-year-olds or one eighty-year-old man?'

She answered, 'I think two twenty-two-year-olds better than men of eighty.'

'You will pay for these words, you whore,' said Hjalti, and he went up to her and bit off her nose.[76] 'You can blame me if anyone fights over you, but I expect that from now on, most will think you scarcely a treasure.'

'You treat me miserably,' she said, 'and it is undeserved.'

'Everyone,' said Hjalti, 'can be fooled by scheming.'

Hjalti then reached for his weapons, because he saw that the area around the stronghold was packed with men in armour, and that war standards had been raised. Realizing that battle was at hand, he made his way to the hall where King Hrolf sat with his champions.

'Wake up, my lord king,' said Hjalti,[77] 'War has come into our courtyard. The need is more for fighting than for fondling women. The gold in the hall will, I think, be little increased by the tribute from your sister Skuld. She has the fierceness of the Skoldungs, and I can tell you that it is no small army, with swords drawn and other weapons ready, which circles the fortress. King Hjorvard has not come on a friendly errand, nor has he any intention from now on of seeking your permission to rule his own kingdom.

'Now is the time,' said Hjalti, 'for us to lead the forces of our king, that man who denies us nothing. Let us fulfil our solemn vows that we will defend the king who has become the most famous in all the northern lands. Let it be heard in every land how we repaid him for the weapons, armour and many other generous acts, because what faces us will not be a minor undertaking. We have for a long time, despite many clear indications, ignored what was coming. Now I have reason to suspect that momentous events, of the type that will long be remembered, are about to take place. Some might say that I perhaps speak from fear, but it may be that King Hrolf drinks for the last time with his champions and his retainers.

'Rise now, all you champions,' said Hjalti, 'and be quick about parting from your mistresses. Other matters are staring you in the face. Prepare yourselves for what is about to happen. Up, all you champions! Everyone must arm himself at once.'

Then Hromund the Hard leapt up, followed by Hrolf the Swift-Handed, Svipdag and Beygad, and Hvitserk the Bold. Haklang was the sixth, Hardrefil the seventh, Haki the Valiant the eighth, Vott the Arrogant the ninth and Storolf was the name of the tenth. Hjalti the Magnanimous was the eleventh and Bodvar Bjarki was the twelfth.

Bodvar was so named because he drove out King Hrolf's bullying and unjust berserkers. Some he killed and none of them was successful against him. In comparison to him, the berserkers, when put to the test, were like children. Nevertheless, they always considered themselves superior, and they continually plotted against Bodvar.

Bodvar Bjarki immediately stood up. He put on his war gear and said that King Hrolf now badly needed brave men: 'Heart and courage will be required of all those who choose to stand alongside King Hrolf, rather than to hide behind him.'

Then King Hrolf sprang to his feet. Showing not a trace of fear, he began to speak, 'Let us now down the finest drink that can be had. We do it before the battle, making us cheerful, and in this way we show what manner of men Hrolf's champions are. Let us strive only to make our bravery so superior that it will never be forgotten, because gathered here are the finest and most courageous champions from all the surrounding lands. Tell Hjorvard and Skuld and their men that we will drink to our satisfaction before setting out to take the tribute.'

The king's orders were obeyed. Skuld answered, 'King Hrolf, my brother, is unlike all others, and the loss of such men is a dreadful misfortune. Nevertheless, all now moves towards the same end.' So highly was King Hrolf regarded that he was praised by both friends and enemies.

## 33. The Great Battle

After drinking for a while, King Hrolf leapt up from the high seat, and all his champions followed his example. They left the pleasing drink and immediately went outside, everyone, that is, except Bodvar Bjarki. He was nowhere to be seen, a fact that greatly perplexed the others. They thought it possible that Bodvar had been captured or killed.

As soon as they went outside, a furious battle began. King Hrolf pushed forward with his standard. He was accompanied on both sides by his champions and by all the men of the stronghold. These latter were not few in number, even if they did not count for much in battle. Much was to be seen: massive blows struck helmets and mail coats while swords and spears flashed in the air. So numerous were the corpses that the ground was entirely covered with them.

Hjalti the Magnanimous said, 'Many mail coats are now slit open and many weapons are broken; helmets are smashed and brave knights are thrown from their mounts. Our king is in fine humour, for now he is as cheerful as when drinking deepest of his ale. He strikes alike with both hands, and in battle he is unlike other kings. To me he seems to have the strength of twelve men, so many brave men has he killed. Now King Hjorvard can see that the sword Skofnung cuts; it rings loudly within their skulls.' The nature of Skofnung was such that it sang aloud when it struck bone.

The battle now became so fierce that nothing could withstand King Hrolf and his champions. Skofnung in hand, King Hrolf fought in a way that seemed a marvel. His courage made a great impression on King Hjorvard's army, whose men fell in heaps.

Hjorvard and his men saw a great bear advancing in front of King Hrolf's troop. The bear was always beside the king, and it killed more men with its paw than any five of the king's champions did. Blows and missiles glanced off the animal, as it used its weight to crush King Hjorvard's men and their horses. Between its teeth, it tore everything within reach, causing a palpable fear to spread through the ranks of King Hjorvard's army.

Hjalti looked around for his companion Bodvar but did not see him. He said to King Hrolf, 'What does it mean when Bodvar looks to his own safety and does not stand beside the king? We thought him such a champion, which indeed he has often proven himself to be.'

King Hrolf answered, 'Bodvar will be where he serves us best, if it is he who decides. Look to your own pride and prowess and do not reproach him, because not one of you is his equal. I do not hold this disparity against any of you, because you are all the most courageous of champions.'

Hjalti now ran back to the king's chamber, where he found Bodvar sitting idle.[78] Hjalti spoke, 'How long shall we wait for this most famous of men? It is a major disgrace that you are not on your feet. You should be testing the strength of your arms, which are as strong as a bear's. Get up now, Bodvar Bjarki, my master, otherwise I will burn down the house and you in it. There is dishonour in this conduct for such a champion as you. While the king endangers his life for us, you lose the renown that you have for so long enjoyed.'

Then Bodvar stood up. He sighed deeply and said, 'You need not try to frighten me, Hjalti, because I have not yet begun to be afraid, but now I am quite prepared to go. When I was young I fled from neither fire not steel. Fire have I seldom tested, although the passage of steel weapons is something that I have endured. Until now, I have survived both. You can in truth say that I wish to fight at my utmost level. King Hrolf has always called me a champion in front of his men. I have also many other things to repay. First there is our bond by marriage and the twelve estates that he gave me; and then there are the many valuable gifts. I killed the berserker Agnar, a man of no lesser rank than that of a king, and that deed is well remembered.' Bodvar now recounted for Hjalti many of his remarkable feats, noting that he had killed many men. He asked Hjalti, therefore, to recognize that he went into battle without fear, adding, 'Although I think that in this current battle we are grappling with something far stranger than either of us has ever experienced. But you, Hjalti, by disturbing me here, have not been as helpful to the king as you think you have. It was nearly decided which side had gained the victory. You have acted more out of ignorance than out of enmity to the king. Among the king's champions there is no one except you whom I would have permitted to call me out, as you have done. Anyone else, except for the king himself, I would have killed. Now events will run their course, turning out as they will, and no action on our part will affect the outcome. In truth, I can tell you that in many ways I can now offer the king far less support than before you woke me.'

Hjalti responded, 'It is clear that my concern is for you and King Hrolf. Yet it is difficult to make the right decision when events develop as they have.'

After Hjalti's challenge, Bodvar stood up and went out to the battle. The bear was gone from King Hrolf's force, and now the battle began to turn against the king. Queen Skuld, from where she sat in her black tent on the witch's scaffold, had been unable to work any magic while the bear was in King Hrolf's ranks.

The situation then changed as much as when dark night follows a bright day. King Hrolf's men now saw a hideous boar advancing from King Hjorvard's force. In size it appeared to be no smaller than a three-year-old bull. Its colour was wolf-grey. An arrow shot out from each of its bristles and, in a monstrous way, it mowed down King Hrolf's retainers in droves.

Hewing with both hands, Bodvar Bjarki moved forcefully around. He thought of nothing else but to cause as much damage as possible before he fell. Men fell dead across each other in front of him, until both his shoulders were covered with blood. Corpses were heaped high all around him, and he behaved as though overcome with madness. However many of Hjorvard's and Skuld's men he and Hrolf's champions killed, their enemies' ranks, remarkably, never diminished. It was as though Hrolf's men were having no effect, and they thought they had never come upon so strange an occurrence.

Bodvar said, 'Deep are the ranks of Skuld's army. I suspect that the dead are wandering about. They rise up again to fight against us, and it becomes difficult to fight with ghosts.[79] As many limbs as we cleave, shields as we split, helmets and mail coats as we hew apart, and war leaders we cut down, the encounters with the dead are the grimmest. We lack the strength to combat such opponents. But where is that champion of King Hrolf who most questioned my courage and, until I answered him, repeatedly challenged me to enter the fight? I do not see him now, and it is not often that I criticize others.'

Then Hjalti said, 'You speak truthfully, and you are not a man to slander others. Here stands the man named Hjalti, but I still have some work to do. There is not much distance between us, and I could use the support of good men, foster brother, because all my armour has been hacked off me. Even though I believe that I am fighting to my limit, I am no longer able to avenge all the blows I have received. But now we must hold nothing back, if we are to be guests this evening in Valhalla.[80] Certainly we have never come up against a marvel such as we now face, although we have long been forewarned about the events now occurring.'

Bodvar said, 'Listen to my words. I have fought in twelve pitched battles. Always I have been called fearless and have never given way to a berserker. It was I who encouraged King Hrolf to seek out King Adils in his home. We were met with deceit, but that was nothing compared to this foulness. My heart is now so gripped by these events that my eagerness to continue the fight has diminished. A short while ago, in the earlier clash, I was up against King Hjorvard. We were face to face, and neither of us threw insults at the other, although we exchanged blows for a time. He gave me a blow that I found heavy, while I, for my part, hacked off a hand and a foot. I landed another blow on his shoulder, slicing him down his side, for the length of his spine. His reaction was not even to sigh. It was as if he dozed for a time, and I thought him dead. Few men like him are to be found, for he fought afterward no less boldly than before, and I cannot say what it is that is driving him. Assembled here against us are many men, rich and powerful, pouring in from all directions, so that there is no defence. I do not recognize Odin among them, although I strongly suspect that this foul and unfaithful son of the evil one will be hovering in the background and causing us harm.[81] If someone would only point him out to me I would squeeze him like a detestable puny mouse. That vile, poisonous creature would be shamelessly treated if I could just get my hands on him. Who would not have bitterness in his heart if he saw his liege lord as ill treated as we now see ours.'

Hjalti answered, 'It is not possible to bend fate, nor can one stand against nature.' At this point they ceased their talk.

## 34. *The Death of King Hrolf Kraki*

King Hrolf defended himself well, fighting resolutely and with more courage than has been told of any man. He was attacked relentlessly, and a select company of King Hjorvard's and Skuld's warriors formed a ring around him. Skuld now entered into the fray. She fiercely incited her rabble to attack King Hrolf because she saw that the champions were no longer close beside him. Bodvar Bjarki sorely grieved that he was unable to assist his lord. The other champions felt the same regret. All of them were now as willing to die with King Hrolf as they had been to live with him, when they were in the full vigour of their youth.

By now all of the king's bodyguard had fallen. Not one of them was left standing, and most of the champions were mortally wounded.

'And events turned out as expected,' said Master Galterus.[82] 'Human strength cannot withstand such fiendish power, unless the strength of God is employed against it. That alone stood between you and victory, King Hrolf,' said the Master; 'you had no knowledge of your Creator.'

Such a storm of enchantments now descended upon them that the champions began to fall, one across the other. King Hrolf managed to emerge from behind the shield wall, but he was nearly dead from exhaustion. There is no need to draw out the tale. King Hrolf fell gloriously, together with all his champions. They made so much of a slaughter there that words alone are inadequate to describe it. King Hjorvard and all his army fell, save only a few shirkers who, together with Skuld, were still on their feet.

Skuld took all of King Hrolf's realm under her power, but she ruled poorly and for only a short time. Elk-Frodi set out to avenge his brother Bodvar Bjarki as he had promised to do. He was joined by King Thorir Hound's Foot, as is told in Elk-Frodi's tale. The brothers were supported by a strong contingent sent from the Swedish kingdom by Queen Yrsa, and men say that Vogg served as the commander. All of these forces sailed for Denmark, and Skuld was taken by surprise. They seized and held her in such a way that she was prevented from working any witchcraft. They killed all of her rabble and tortured her in different ways. The kingdoms returned to the rule of King Hrolf's daughters. When all this had been accomplished, everyone went home.

A burial mound was raised for King Hrolf, and the sword Skofnung was laid in the mound with him. A mound was raised for each of the champions, and they likewise were buried with their weapons.

And here ends the saga of King Hrolf Kraki and his champions.

# Notes

*The Saga of King Hrolf Kraki* is an unusually rich cultural document. These notes are designed for the reader who wants additional information on sorcery and magic, the meaning of Old Norse terms and the relationship between *Hrolf's Saga* and other medieval Scandinavian and English texts treating related characters and events.

**1.** King Halfdan is known from several medieval sources. His name, meaning 'Half-Dane', corresponds to that of the Danish king Healfdene, who is mentioned in the Old English poem *Beowulf* as the son of an early king called Beowulf the Dane, who is not to be confused with the epic's hero, Beowulf. In the Latin *Saga of the Skjoldungs* Halfdan, identified as Frodi's son, is slain by his brother, Ingialldus (Old Norse Ingjaldr), who corresponds to the Old English Ingeld.

**2.** In *Beowulf*, Healfdene's unnamed daughter marries the Swedish king Onela, who corresponds to Ali in Old Norse tradition. Ali, though not mentioned in *Hrolf's Saga*, appears in other Scandinavian versions of these events.

**3.** The genealogy of Halfdan and his sons was also recorded by the thirteenth-century Danish historian Saxo Grammaticus in his *History of the Danes*. Old English literature attributes three sons to Healfdene: Heorogar, Hrothgar and Halga. Hrothgar, the king in *Beowulf*, and Halga clearly correspond to the Old Norse Hroar and Helgi. Heorogar, however, is not mentioned in the Scandinavian sources.

**4.** Fosterage was the custom of having a child raised in another household in order to extend kinship bonds or to form political alliances.

**5.** The term *karl* denotes a freeman. Depending on usage, it can mean a freeholding farmer, similar to an English yeoman, as here in the instance of Vifil. Later in the saga the term is used to denote lower social classes, particularly servants and poor farmers, unsuitable to marry into a king's family.

**6.** *Vifill*, meaning 'beetle', was a name commonly given to slaves or freedmen.

7. Old Norse *jarðhús* means 'earth house' or 'underground house', i.e. some form of a dugout or perhaps originally a cave.

8. *Völur* (sibyls or seeresses) and *vísindamenn* (soothsayers or wise men) were persons whose 'wisdom' or supernaturally obtained knowledge was derived from mastery of ancient lore, including songs, spells and incantations. Such people, especially women, often practised *seiðr*, a form of magic involving rituals and trances with many shamanistic elements. A characteristic of *seiðr* was that it allowed the practitioner to divine the future and to see into the hidden.

9. *Galdramenn* (sorcerers) were magicians and wizards. *Galdr* was a type of magic based on spells, whether spoken, sung or carved in runes. It was distinct from the more shamanistic *seiðr*, which involved ecstatic trances. These 'sorcerers' should be differentiated from the soothsayers (wise men) mentioned earlier.

10. *Fylgjur* (fetches) were usually conceived of as guardian spirits attached to individuals or families. They often appear in dreams or at the moment of death. Here they are more akin to the 'sendings' of later Icelandic folklore: malevolent spirits under the direct control of a master magician or sorcerer. They may be seen as shadows of the sorcerer himself.

11. *Hrani*, which means 'blusterer', occasionally occurs as a personal name in thirteenth-century Iceland. It is also, as in chapter 26 of this saga, one of the many names used for the god Odin. *Ham*, meaning 'shape' or 'skin', can metaphorically be interpreted as 'frame of mind'.

12. A complex verse, meaning that the trunk of the tree, that is the father, has been taken away, leaving only limbs, that is the children.

13. Heid is a *völva* who will practise *seiðr*. Heid is also the name of the Sibyl in the Eddic poem *Völuspá*, 'The Sibyl's Prophecy'.

14. The *seiðhjallr* (trance platform) was a platform or scaffold, usually built of timber, on which the Sibyl would sit to perform her *seiðr*. The most complete description of a *seiðr* ceremony is found in *The Saga of Eirik the Red*, but it does not mention a *seiðhjallr*; instead, the Sibyl sits in the host's high seat.

15. The phrase is literally 'wolves among the wolves' (*vargar með úlfum*). *Vargr* (wolf) was a term applied to dangerous outlaws, who could be hunted down like wolves.

16. Hroar thus takes an English wife. In *Beowulf*, Hroar's equivalent Hrothgar is said to have married Wealhtheow, whose name suggests that she, like Ogn, was of foreign origin.

17. Translated here as 'lands', the word *ríki* has the connotation of independent state or kingdom.

18. Old Norse *Ólöf* is the feminine form of the common (masculine) personal name Olaf. Although not otherworldly, this warrior queen has some of the

characteristics of the legendary shield-maidens or Valkyries, supernatural female warriors mentioned in other Scandinavian sagas and poems.

19. *Kurteisi* (courtesy) was a thirteenth-century borrowing from Old French. The concept was originally foreign to Scandinavia.

20. The name Yrsa, unusual in medieval Norse narrative, may derive from Latin *ursa* (she-bear). Saxo gives her name as 'Vrsa'. In the *Lejre Chronicle* (*c.* 1170) she has the Latin name 'Ursula'. Although the name does not appear in Anglo-Saxon sources, many scholars change the text of *Beowulf*, line 62a, where the manuscript is defective, to read, 'I heard Yrse was Onela's queen.' The addition is based largely on *Hrolf's Saga*.

21. In *The Saga of the Skjoldungs*, Agnar's story is somewhat different. He is the son of Ingjald, hence a cousin (rather than son) to Hroar and half-brother (rather than cousin) to Hrok. He is later killed by Bjarki, a retainer of Hrolf, and the ring returns to Yrsa.

22. Concerning Hrolf, see the Introduction. Hrolf appears in *Beowulf* as Hrothulf, who shares the Danish kingdom with Hrothgar.

23. In *Beowulf* Adils appears as Eadgils and is identified as the nephew of Onela (Ali), the husband of Healfdene's unnamed daughter. According to Snorri Sturluson's *Saga of the Ynglings* (*Ynglinga Saga*), Adils carried off Yrsa, the daughter of Olof. Helgi subsequently recaptured her from Adils, but she returned to Adils when the incest was revealed.

24. Yule, the pre-Christian winter feast later assimilated to Christmas, was an occasion for drinking bouts, swearing of oaths and general merrymaking. In Scandinavia the event is frequently associated with supernatural encounters.

25. Elves (*álfar*) were supernatural beings associated with the fertility gods. In Scandinavia they were often portrayed as human-sized, attractive beings with sometimes vindictive natures. The story here is reminiscent of late Icelandic folk traditions.

26. Berserkers (*berserkir*) are frequently mentioned in the sagas. Scholars disagree as to whether berserkers existed or were primarily a literary creation, and no consensus exists regarding the word's etymology. Berserkers are discussed in the Introduction.

27. The word *fiölkyngi*, here translated as 'sorcery', literally means 'very cunning' and also refers to 'the black arts' and 'witchcraft'. The word often had negative connotations, especially when contrasted with the more neutral *galdr*, even though the two terms are sometimes used interchangeably. The author of *Hrolf's Saga*, a Christian writing for a Christian audience, tends to use such terms pejoratively.

28. Svipdag is elsewhere given as a name for Odin. In *Hrolf's Saga* many traits commonly associated with Odin are attributed to Svipdag, although it is not

clear that the author intended Svipdag to be positively identified with the god. It is possible that the underlying connection reflects an older form of the story.

**29.** One of the sons of the legendary warrior Ragnar Hairy-Breeches was also called Hvitserk, meaning 'White-shirt'.

**30.** This statement resembles advice given in the Eddic poem *Hávamál*, 'The Sayings of the High One'.

**31.** These games were usually tests of strength, such as lifting competitions, single combat or tug-of-war.

**32.** The saga employs the word *hólmganga*, one of several forms of single combat with strict rules. The term means 'island going' because a small delineated space, often an island, was chosen as the site for such combats.

**33.** Old Norse *herspori* (war-spur) seems to be a kind of caltrop, a ball with four spikes protruding from it in such a way that no matter how it is dropped three spikes form a base while the fourth points upward.

**34.** Svipdag thus resembles Odin, who had only one eye, having sacrificed the other for wisdom and power. The attribute also connects Svipdag with the legendary Swedish king Svipdag the Blind from *The Saga of the Ynglings*.

**35.** Modern Lejre. See Introduction.

**36.** Hjorvard corresponds to *Beowulf*'s Heoroweard, the son of Heorogar and Hrothulf's cousin. In *Beowulf*, Heoroweard had a strong claim to the throne, one cause for the enmity between him and Hrothulf. This element is lacking in the saga.

**37.** *Uppdalir* means inland, often highland, valleys. There are several places in Norway that this might refer to, among them a region near Trondheim and a region north of Oslo Fjord.

**38.** Bjorn (Bear) was, and still is, a common personal name.

**39.** Finnmark, 'the Borderland of the Finns', is modern Lapland. The people known as Finns to the Old Norse speakers were the ancestors of the modern Saami, and they had a reputation for magic and witchcraft. The name 'Finn' is often used synonymously with 'sorcerer'.

**40.** *Bera* means 'She-bear'.

**41.** Skin gloves were often part of the paraphernalia of a sorceress. The sibyl in *The Saga of Eirik the Red* is said to have had gloves made of white catskin.

**42.** Humanlike eyes were a sign that animals either were enchanted humans or were possessed by the spirits of the dead.

**43.** *Tröll* had a broader meaning in Old Norse than it does in Modern English usage. It designated a variety of harmful supernatural creatures, including fiends, ghosts, witches and giants.

**44.** Runes were the alphabet used by the Germanic peoples for writing on bone, wood, metal and stone. In addition to practical uses, runes had magical properties.

45. Elk-Frodi (*Elgfróði*) means 'Elk-wise'.

46. Bodvar means 'warlike', and *Bjarki* means 'little bear'. See the Introduction. According to Saxo's version of the *Lay of Bjarki*, Bjarki won the epithet 'warlike' as a result of killing Agnar.

47. In the Icelandic rhymed poem *Bjarkarímur*, Bodvar is said to have been born with a bear's claw on his toe.

48. The Old Norse word is *hildr*, a poetic term for battle and also a Valkyrie's name. The poet is playing on this double meaning, drawing attention to the Valkyrie's work, that is warfare. Hild is a common element in Germanic women's names.

49. The Gauts correspond to the Geats of *Beowulf*. Beowulf himself was a Geat and later became their king.

50. Stories featuring less than affectionate stepmothers were well known to medieval Icelanders, who referred to them as 'stepmother tales'.

51. Though sounding modern, street (*stræti*) was an Old Norse word, referring to a road within a town. Probably of Latin origin, the word was in current usage by the twelfth century and perhaps earlier. It may have been a borrowing from Old English.

52. This sword, if difficult to control (see chap. 23, where Bodvar has difficulty drawing his weapon), has many otherwise typical attributes of magic swords in Old Norse legend. In *The Saga of King Heidrek the Wise*, for example, the blows of the sword Tyrfing would never go astray and the sword could never be drawn without bringing about the death of a man; it was cursed to cause three hateful acts. In the *Prose Edda*, Snorri mentions a sword with similar properties, called Dainsleif, 'Dain's heirloom'.

53. The proper term for the now functionless digit on the foot of some animals is 'dewclaw'.

54. Throwing bones was apparently one of the rowdier games played at feasts, and killing by bone-throwing is specifically listed as an offence in a number of medieval Scandinavian law codes. Sven Aggesen, who wrote in the twelfth century, reports that, according to the law of the Danish King Knut, any bodyguard who broke the law was required to sit lower than the other bodyguards, thus allowing the others to pelt him with bones.

55. According to Saxo's *History*, this episode took place at the wedding of Hrolf's sister to Agnar Ingjaldsson.

56. Much as no weapon can injure the dragon which ravages Hleidargard each Yule, Grendel, in *Beowulf*, cannot be killed with a sword.

57. This episode shows close parallels with both *Beowulf* and the fight between

Grettir and Glam in *Grettir's Saga*. The motif of the monster who is impervious to human weapons is common in legends and folktales, as well as in the sagas, and its presence in both *Beowulf* and *Hrolf's Saga* does not necessarily imply a direct connection between the texts.

**58**. The same phrase, *mesta tröll* (greatest troll), was earlier applied to Bodvar's treacherous stepmother, Hvit. Elsewhere in this current episode, the monster is referred to simply as a *dýr* (animal or beast). The wings of the monster may represent an innovation on the part of the saga's Icelandic author.

**59**. Eating a part of an animal or drinking its blood in order to acquire its nature, whether good or bad, is a common motif. The same belief lies at the root of two earlier episodes in the saga: Bodvar's acquisition of strength and prowess through drinking the blood of his brother Elk-Frodi (chap. 23) and the animal-like attributes of Bera's children as a result of her eating bearmeat while pregnant (chap. 20). The present episode is thematically similar to one in *The Saga of the Volsungs*, in which Sigurd gains wisdom by drinking the blood and eating the heart of the dragon Fafnir. There are also Irish parallels, among them the many stories of Fionn mac Cumhail.

**60**. The Old Norse name for the sword is *Gullinn-hjalti* (Golden Hilt). The sword that Beowulf finds in the underwater lair of Grendel's mother is referred to as *gylden-hilt*, although it is unclear whether this is meant as a proper name. The word 'hilt' refers in Old English and Old Norse to different parts of the sword. In English it is the part which one grasps, whereas in Old Norse it refers either to the guard piece between the hilt and the blade or to the boss or knob at the end of the sword's hilt. Hrolf usually carried a different sword, named Skofnung.

**61**. In Saxo's account, no similar name-change occurs. Hjalti remains Hjalti throughout the text.

**62**. Earlier in the saga (chap. 15), Hrolf is said to have two daughters, Skur and Drifa.

**63**. Adils is Hrolf's brother-in-law as well as his father-in-law.

**64**. *The Saga of the Skjoldungs*, Snorri in his *Prose Edda* and Saxo all give somewhat different reasons for Hrolf's expedition to Sweden. In Saxo's account, for example, Yrsa pretends to conspire with her husband, luring Hrolf to Sweden with gifts while desiring that Hrolf help her flee.

**65**. Hrani is an alias of Odin. In chapter 3 Helgi assumes the name Hrani to conceal his true identity, although he has no apparent connection with Odin.

**66**. Terms of courtesy such as 'chivalrous knights' are of foreign origin, reflecting the literary influence of courtly romances from the Continent.

**67**. *Kraki* means 'pole ladder' or 'stake'. Saxo Grammaticus explains that the word refers to a tree trunk trimmed so that it can be used as a ladder. Both *The*

*Saga of the Skjoldungs* and Snorri's *Prose Edda* report the name-giving incident and Hrolf's expedition to Sweden as two unrelated events. In *The Saga of the Skjoldungs*, the name *kraki* is explained as derived from the Danish *krag*, 'sea-crow'.

**68**. *Gram* (wrathful) is also the name of the sword reforged for Sigurd in *The Saga of the Volsungs*.

**69**. In Scandinavian mythology, the boar was sacred to the fertility god Freyr, who was considered the ancestor of the Swedish royal house, and the boar was used iconographically to represent both Freyr and Sweden. The boar was also a symbol of ferocity and virility, appearing as decoration on numerous artifacts, for example the boar helmets found at Sutton Hoo and Vendel.

**70**. *Svíagrís* means 'Pig of the Swedes'. According to *The Saga of the Skjoldungs*, this ring had been taken from the Swedes as booty by one of King Hrolf's Danish forebears.

**71**. Snorri Sturluson relates this episode in the *Prose Edda* to explain why the phrases 'Kraki's seed' and 'the seed of the Fyris Plains' are used as metaphors or kennings for gold.

**72**. Although Odin is here treated as malevolent by the Christian scribe or author, his traditional pre-Christian function as the stranger who grants victory has not changed.

**73**. This again appears to be a Christian rationalization of the evil nature of pagan creatures.

**74**. The Christian writer may be building up Hrolf's pride as sinful conduct, blinding him from attending to matters at hand. Some of these Christian interjections may come from a later scribe.

**75**. Several saga characters, both historical and legendary, are said to have ignored pagan worship and relied on their own 'might and main'.

**76**. This episode makes more sense in Saxo's version. There Hjalti does not see Skuld's army until after he has been with his mistress. He does not question her; rather, she asks him whether she should marry a young or an old man, if he is killed in the battle. The motivation for cutting off the nose is unclear. Probably he is punishing her for holding his attention while he should be alerting Hrolf, but it may also reflect some sort of punishment for an adultery occurring in an earlier version of the story.

**77**. The long, stylized speeches in this chapter and the following one are apparently paraphrases of stanzas from the mostly lost poem *Bjarkamál*, 'The Lay of Bjarki'.

**78**. Bodvar is almost certainly in a shaman-like trance, carrying out the acts of the bear fighting beside King Hrolf.

**79**. Ghosts (*draugar*) in Icelandic tradition are not ethereal spirits, but rather corporeal creatures returned from the dead (see, for example, *Grettir's Saga*).

**80**. *Valhöll* is mentioned in both *The Prose Edda* and *The Poetic Edda*. Warriors who die bravely in battle, whether on the winning or on the losing side, are taken by valkyries to Odin's hall, Valhalla. There they train for the final battle at Ragnarok, while enjoying perpetual feasting and celebration.

**81**. The term used is 'the Son of Herjan' (*sonrinn Herjans*). In the *Poetic Edda*, *Herjan* is a name for Odin meaning 'Lord of Hosts'. In later Icelandic usage *Herjan* came to mean 'the Evil One', a term of abuse, and *Herjan's son* meant a 'Devil's limb'.

**82**. Galterus is Walter of Chatillon (*c.* 1135–1203/04). He wrote a Latin epic on the life of Alexander the Great that was translated into Icelandic prose as *Alexander's Saga*. The author's or the scribe's reason for introducing this reference at this point in the story is unclear.

# Genealogical Tables

# The Family of King Hrolf Kraki

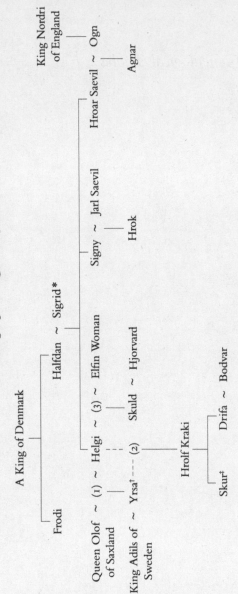

King Nordri of England

A King of Denmark

Halfdan ~ Sigrid*

King Nordri of England — Ogn

Hroar Saevil

Signy ~ Jarl Saevil

Agnar

Hrok

Frodi

Queen Olof of Saxland ~ (1) ~ Helgi ~ (3) ~ Elfin Woman

Skuld ~ Hjorvard

King Adils of Sweden ~ Yrsa† --- (2)

Hrolf Kraki

Skur‡    Drifa ~ Bodvar

The numbers in parentheses in the above chart represent the chronological order of marriages and liaisons.

According to the saga, Helgi had offspring first with Queen Olof, next with Queen Yrsa and then with the Elfin Woman

\* Sigrid is only mentioned as the mother of Helgi and Hroar; she may not be Signy's mother.

† Yrsa is both the daughter and wife of Helgi.

‡ The number of Hrolf's daughters is ambiguous. Drifa, when given to Bodvar in marriage (chapter 24), is referred to as Hrolf's 'only daughter'. Earlier (chapter 15), Skur is also identified as Hrolf's daughter.

# The Family of Bodvar Bjarki

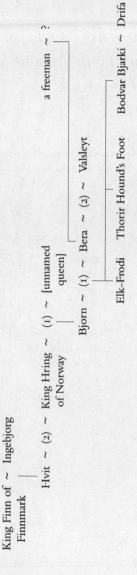

King Finn of ~ Ingebjorg
Finnmark

Hvit ~ (2) ~ King Hring ~ (1) ~ [unnamed
of Norway          queen]

Bjorn ~ (1) ~ Bera ~ (2) ~ Valsleyt

a freeman ~ ?

Elk-Frodi    Thorir Hound's Foot    Bodvar Bjarki ~ Drifa

# The Family of Svipdag

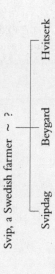

Svip, a Swedish farmer ~ ?

Svipdag    Beygard    Hvitserk

# Equivalent Characters in Old Norse, Old English and Latin Accounts of King Hrolf Kraki

This table is designed to assist the reader in comparing different versions of the story of King Hrolf Kraki by providing a quick means of identifying equivalent characters in the Old Norse *Hrólfs Saga*, the Old English *Bēowulf*, Saxo Grammaticus's Latin *Gesta Danorum (History of the Danes)* and the Latin paraphrase of the Old Norse *Skjöldunga Saga*.

| *Hrólfs Saga* | *Skjöldunga Saga* | *Gesta Danorum* | *Bēowulf* |
|---|---|---|---|
| Aðils | Adillus | Athislus | Ēadgils |
| Böðvarr Bjarki | Bodvarus | Biarco | Bēowulf* |
| Fróði | Frodo | Frotho | Frōda |
| Hálfdan | Halfdanus | Haldanus | Healfdene |
| Helgi | Helgo | Helgo | Hālga |
| Hróarr | Roas | Roe | Hrōðgār |
| Hrólfr Kraki | Rolfo Krake | Roluo Krake | Hrōðulf |
| Skjöldr | Skioldus | Skioldus | Scyld Scēfing |
| Yrsa | Yrsa | Vrsa | Yrse* |

* Probable associations.

# Glossary of Proper Names

This glossary has been compiled to provide the reader with a tool for locating the people (both human and supernatural), groups, places, animals and objects that appear in *The Saga of King Hrolf Kraki*. Entries are alphabetized. Numbers refer to the chapters in the saga. When entries appear in brackets it signifies that the character plays an important part in the chapter without being explicitly named there.

ADILS: King of Sweden, marries Yrsa, 11; treacherously ambushes and kills Helgi, 12; gloats over Helgi's death, 13; takes champion Svipdag into his retinue, but abandons Svipdag in battle against berserkers, 14; Hrolf wants treasure of Helgi which Adils has, 15; mentioned 16, 33; Bodvar incites Hrolf to get treasure from him, 25; Hrolf's champions tested by Hrani to prepare them to meet Adils, 26; when Hrolf and his champions come to his hall, he uses magic against them and has armed men treacherously attack them, 27; has fires built up to try to scorch Hrolf and his men, 28; sends a boar against them, 28; attempts to burn them in the house, 28; has Hrolf and his men attacked, but hides himself, 29; pursues Hrolf, 29; stoops to pick up the ring Sviagris which Hrolf has thrown down, and Hrolf cuts off his buttocks, 30.

AGNAR: son of Hroar and Ogn, 9; becomes a famous warrior, 9; retrieves ring that was thrown into the sea, 9.

AGNAR: a berserker killed by Bodvar, 33.

BERA: a farmer's daughter, loved by Bjorn, 18; meets Bjorn, now a were-bear, 20; receives the ring that is under Bjorn's shoulder when he is killed in bear form, 20; forced by Hvit to eat some of the bear's flesh, 20; gives birth to Bjorn's sons Elk-Frodi, Thorir and Bodvar, 20; gives sons their father's legacy, 20; reveals to Bodvar and to King Hring the story of Bjorn's death, shows ring as proof, 22; marries Valsleyt, 22.

BEYGAD: son of Svip, who sends him to help his brother Svipdag, in dire straits in battle with berserkers, 14; [goes with Svipdag to join King Hrolf, 15]; in Hrolf's retinue, 24; accompanies Hrolf to Adils' hall, 27; holds the horn, 30; called by Hjalti to Hrolf's final battle, 32.

BJALKI: a man in King Hrolf's retinue, 15.

BJORN: son of King Hring of Uppdales in Norway, 17; loves Bera, 18; remains at home with Queen Hvit while his father goes raiding, 18; turned into a bear by Hvit, who is angry because he rejected her advances, 19; Bjorn, now a were-bear, meets Bera, 20; he tells her of his impending death and of the sons they will have, 20; he is killed in bear-form, 20; Bera and Bodvar reveal the story of his death and punish Hvit for it, 22.

BODVAR BJARKI: son of Bjorn and Bera, 20; tortures and kills Hvit to avenge his father Bjorn, 22; succeeds Hring as king, 22; draws from a rock the sword left him by his father, 23; visits Elk-Frodi, receives a strengthening drink of Elk-Frodi's blood, 23; visits Thorir, 23; joins King Hrolf's retinue, 23; rescues Hott from mistreatment by Hrolf's retainers, 23; kills monster, makes Hott drink its blood, 23; challenges one of Hrolf's berserkers, 24; accounted Hrolf's greatest champion, 24; marries Hrolf's daughter Drifa, 24; incites Hrolf to reclaim his father's wealth from King Adils, 25; withstands ordeal set by Hrani (Odin), 26; with Hrolf in Adils' hall, 27, 28, 29; realizes that by refusing Odin's gift of weapons, Hrolf has lost victory, 30; called *Bjarki* because he cleared out Hrolf's berserkers, 32; a great bear – his fetch – fights while he sits in the hall, 33; Hjalti rouses him to battle, and the bear disappears, 33; falls in battle against Skuld and Hjorvard, 34.

DENMARK: kingdom of Halfdan, seized by Frodi, 1; kingdom of Helgi, 5, 8, 12; kingdom of Hrolf, 15, 16, 23, 30, 31, 34.

DRIFA: daughter of King Hrolf, 15; married to Bodvar, 24.

ELK-FRODI (FRODI): son of Bjorn and Bera, 20; man above and elk below the navel, 20; draws from rock a short sword left him by his father, 20; becomes an outlaw, 20; advises his brother Thorir how to become king of the Gauts, 21; mentioned, 22; Bodvar visits him in disguise, 23; they wrestle until Elk-Frodi recognizes Bodvar; 23; advises Bodvar to join Hrolf's champions, 23; gives Bodvar a strengthening drink of his blood, 23; avenges Bodvar, 34.

ENGLAND: Nordri king there, 5; Hroar settles there, 5.

FINN: King of Finnmark, father of Hvit, 17.

FINNMARK: Hring's men, searching for a bride for him, come ashore in Finnmark, where they find Hvit, 17.

FRODI: king who seizes Denmark from his brother Halfdan, 1; unsuccessfully searches for Hroar and Helgi, 2; discovers identity of Hroar and Helgi when they come to his hall in Saevil's train, 3; burned in his hall by Hroar and Helgi, Regin and Saevil, 4.

FRODI- see ELK-FRODI.

FYRIS PLAINS: Hrolf scatters gold on the Fyris Plains, his pursuers stop to retrieve it and are slowed down, 30.

GALTERUS: Master Galterus attributed Hrolf's defeat to the fact that he did not know his Creator (i.e. was a pagan), 34.

GAUTLAND: Thorir Hound's Foot becomes king there, 21; Bodvar visits Thorir in Gautland, 23.

GAUTS: only the man who can fill a large chair can become their king – Thorir Hound's Foot does so, 21.

GOLDEN HILT (*Gullinn-hjalti*): Hrolf's sword, which he gives to Hott, renaming him Hjalti in its honour, 23.

GRAM: Hrolf's dog, fells monstrous boar sent by Adils, 28.

HABROK: Hrolf's hawk, 27; [kills all of Adils' hawks, 29].

HAKI, 'the Valiant': one of Hrolf's champions, 32.

HAKLANG: one of Hrolf's champions, 32.

HALFDAN: King of Denmark, defeated and killed by his brother Frodi, 1; mentioned, 2, 3, 4, 5.

HAM: alias under which Hroar conceals his identity, 3.

HARDREFIL: one of Hrolf's champions, 32.

HELGI: son of King Halfdan, 1; hides on Vifil's island from his uncle Frodi, who seeks to destroy him, 2; conceals himself with Jarl Saevil under the name Hrani, 3; follows Saevil to Frodi's hall, 3; escapes to the woods when his identity is revealed, 3; interprets Regin's riddling hints of how to destroy Frodi, 3; burns Frodi in his hall, 4; described as a great warrior, 4; rules over Denmark, 5; attempts to marry warrior queen Olof, is disgraced by her, 6; tricks and rapes Olof in revenge for her earlier insult, 7; marries Yrsa, his daughter by Olof, not knowing her parentage, 7; gives Hroar a valuable ring, 7; refuses Hrok's demands for the ring or a share of the kingdom, 8; Ogn appeals to him to avenge Hroar, who was killed by Hrok, 8; defeats and mutilates Hrok, 9; has son Hrolf by Yrsa, 9; Olof reveals that his marriage to Yrsa is incestuous, and Yrsa leaves him, 10; Helgi mourns her loss, 10; mates with an elfin woman, by whom he has a daughter Skuld, 11; goes to Uppsala to see Yrsa, now married to Adils, 12; treacherously ambushed and killed by Adils, 12; Yrsa reproaches Adils for killing Helgi, 13, 28; Hrolf seeks treasure that belonged to him, now held by Adils, 25, 26; Hrolf gets Helgi's treasure, 29.

HEID: seeress, betrays Hroar and Helgi to Frodi and predicts his death at their hands, 3.

HJALTI (see HOTT): new name given to Hott by Hrolf after Hott 'kills' a monster, 23; challenges Hrolf's berserker, 24; one of Hrolf's greatest champions and given the name 'the Magnanimous', 24; with Hrolf in Adils' hall, 27, 28, 29; mutilates his mistress, 32; gives alarm to Hrolf's champions of attack by Hjorvard and Skuld, 32; rouses Bodvar to battle so that the bear which was Bodvar's fetch disappears, 33.

HJORVARD: marries Skuld, 16; tricked into being subject to Hrolf, 16; incited by Skuld to attack Hrolf, 31; battles Hrolf and his champions, 32, 33; killed, 34.

HLEIDARGARD: Hrolf's royal seat in Denmark, 16, 23, 32.

HO: one of Vifil's two dogs, 1; Vifil calls dogs to warn Hroar and Helgi, 2; seeress reveals that 'Ho' was Helgi, 3.

HOPP: one of Vifil's two dogs, 1; Vifil calls dogs to warn Hroar and Helgi, 2; seeress reveals that 'Hopp' was Hroar, 3.

HOTT (see HJALTI): farmer's son, pelted with bones by Hrolf's retinue, 23; Bodvar rescues him from the bone heap, 23; Bodvar kills a monster and makes him drink its blood, 23; he becomes strong and courageous, 23; they set up the dead monster and Hott 'kills' it a second time in front of Hrolf's retinue, 23; Hrolf gives him a new name, Hjalti, 23.

HRANI: alias under which Helgi conceals his identity, 3.

HRANI (ODIN): tests Hrolf's men with cold, thirst and heat, 26; offers Hrolf weapons, is offended when he refuses, Hrolf then realizes that he was Odin, 30.

HRING: king in Norway, 17; has son Bjorn, 17; marries Hvit, 17; goes out raiding, leaving Bjorn at home with Hvit, 18; Hvit tries to seduce his son Bjorn, 19; urged by Hvit to kill bear (who is Bjorn), 20; gives Bera the ring from the bear's shoulder, 20; mentioned, 21; told the story of Bjorn's death, 22; makes Bodvar his heir, 22; dies, 22.

HROAR: son of King Halfdan, 1; hides on Vifil's island from his uncle Frodi, who seeks to destroy him, 2; conceals himself with Jarl Saevil under the name Ham, 3; follows Saevil to Frodi's hall, 3; escapes into the woods when his identity is revealed, 3; burns Frodi in his hall, 4; described as a mild and gentle man, 4; marries Ogn the daughter of Nordri and settles in England, 5; asks for and receives valuable ring from Helgi, 7; cuts off Hrok's feet when Hrok throws ring into the sea, 8; Hrok kills him in revenge, 8; Helgi takes revenge from him, 9.

HROK: son of Saevil and Signy, 5; demands from Helgi a valuable ring or a third of the kingdom of Denmark, 8; Helgi refuses, saying he has given the ring to Hroar, 8; Hrok asks Hroar to show him the ring, then flings it into the sea, 8; Hroar cuts off Hrok's feet, 8; Hrok, in revenge, kills Hroar and demands that Ogn marry him, 8; defeated and mutilated by Helgi, 9.

HROLF: son of Helgi and Yrsa, 9; mentioned, 11; Svip tells of his fame and that of his champions, 15; Svipdag joins his retinue, 15; tricks Hjorvard into being his subject, 16; Bodvar joins his retinue, 23; he renames Hott, Hjalti, 23; makes peace between his berserkers and Bodvar and Hjalti, now the greatest members of his retinue, 24; incited by Bodvar to reclaim his father's wealth from King Adils, 25; journeys to meet Adils, 26; encounters farmer Hrani (Odin) who tests his men with cold, thirst and heat, 26; enters Adils' hall, 27; his men conceal from Adils which one is Hrolf, 27; Adils attacks with magic and armed men, 27; he repulses attack, 27; Adils builds up fires in hall to scorch him, 28; he leads his men in leaping over fire, 28;

Yrsa welcomes him, 28; Vogg gives him name *kraki* and promises to avenge his death, 28; Adils sends boar to attack him, 28; Adils tries to burn him in the house, 28; escapes from burning hall, 29; fights and fells Adils' men, 29; receives ring Sviagris and much treasure from Yrsa, 29; scatters treasure, so that pursuers stop to pick it up and are slowed down, 30; throws down ring Sviagris, 30; cuts off Adils' buttocks when he stoops to retrieve it, 30; refuses weapons offered him by Hrani, who is Odin – he thereby loses the gift of victory, 30; Skuld plans attack on him, 31; warned by Hjalti of attack, 32; battles Skuld and Hjorvard, 33; killed, 34.

HROLF, 'the Swift-Handed': one of King Hrolf's champions, 32.

HROMUND, 'the Hard': one of Hrolf's champions, 32.

HVIT: daughter of King Finn, 17; taken as bride for King Hring, 17; asks that Bjorn be left home with her while Hring goes raiding, 18; [tries to seduce Bjorn, turns him into a bear when he rejects her, 19]; [urges killing of bear, 20; forces Bera to eat bear's flesh, 20]; tortured and killed by Bodvar, 22.

HVITSERK, 'the bold': son of Svip, who sends him to help his brother Svipdag, in dire straits in battle with berserkers, 14; [goes with Svipdag to join King Hrolf, 15]; in Hrolf's retinue, 24; with Hrolf in Adils' hall, 27; warned by Hjalti of attack by Hjorvard and Skuld, 32.

INGEBJORG: mother of Hvit, 17.

NORDRI: a king in England, 5; Hroar befriends him and marries his daughter Ogn, 5; wants to repulse Hrok, but too old, 8.

NORTHUMBERLAND: land where Hroar rules, 7, 8.

NORWAY: Hring, king in Norway, 17.

ODIN: [a voice (Odin?) welcomes home Frodi and his men, about to be killed, 4]; [as farmer HRANI, tests Hrolf's men with cold, thirst and heat, 26]; as Hrani, offers Hrolf weapons which he refuses, 30; Hrolf then realizes that Hrani was Odin, for he had only one eye, 30; Hrolf has lost the gift of victory henceforth, 30; Bodvar threatens that he would treat Odin abusively if he saw him, 33.

OGN: daughter of Nordri, 5; married to Hroar, 5; Hrok, when he has killed Hroar, seeks to marry her, 8; with child by Hroar, she appeals to Helgi for protection against Hrok, 8; has son Agnar, 9.

OLOF: warrior queen of Saxland, 6; disgraces Helgi when he seeks to marry her, 6; Helgi tricks and rapes Olof in return for her earlier insult to him, 7; she bears a daughter Yrsa by Helgi, 7; spitefully keeps silent about Yrsa's parentage when Helgi marries Yrsa, 7; reveals to Yrsa that she is incestuously married to her father, 10; receives Adils' proposal to marry Yrsa, 11.

REGIN: foster-father of Hroar and Helgi, hides them from Frodi, 1; creates confusion in Frodi's hall to give Hroar and Helgi a chance to escape, 3; gives them riddling hints how to destroy Frodi, 3; 'warns' Frodi in ambiguous punning verse of danger he is in, 4; joins in burning Frodi in his hall, 4; dies, 5; mentioned, 8.

SAEVIL: a jarl, husband of King Halfdan's daughter Signy, 1; Vifil sends Hroar and Helgi into hiding with Saevil, 2; Hroar and Helgi follow him in disguise to Frodi's hall, 3; he attempts to conceal their identity, 3; joins Hroar and Helgi in burning Frodi in his hall, 4; has son Hrok, 5; dies, 8.

SAXLAND: land where warrior queen Olof rules 6, 7, 10; Yrsa takes refuge in Saxland from her incestuous marriage, 10.

SIGNY: daughter of King Halfdan, wife of Jarl Saevil, 1; recognizes her disguised brothers Hroar and Helgi, 3; attempts to forestall seeress from revealing their identity to Frodi, 3; has son Hrok, 5; covets ring that Helgi owns, 7; [incites Hrok to demand ring, 8].

SIGRID: mother of Hroar and Helgi, 4; refuses to leave Frodi's hall and is burned inside, 4.

SKJOLDUNGS: dynasty to which Halfdan, Hroar and Helgi belong, 3; Skuld has fierceness of the Skjoldungs, 32.

SKOFNUNG: sword with which Hrolf cuts off Adils' buttocks, 30; Hrolf fights with Skofnung in battle against Hjorvard and Skuld, 33; it rings when it touches bone, 33; sword buried with Hrolf, 34.

SKULD: Helgi's daughter by an elfin woman, 11; marries Hjorvard, 16; attacks Hrolf, 31, 32; fights Hrolf and his champions with witchcraft, 33; sends a great boar, 33; raises the dead to continue fighting, 33; wins battle, 34; rules Hrolf's kingdom until killed by army said to be led by Vogg, 34.

SKUR: daughter of King Hrolf, 15.

STOROLF: one of Hrolf's champions, 32.

SVIAGRIS, 'pig of the Swedes': a precious ring belonging to Adils, given to Hrolf by Yrsa, 29; Hrolf, pursued by Adils, throws down Sviagris, 30; Adils stoops to retrieve the ring, and Hrolf cuts off his buttocks, 30.

SVIP: Swedish farmer, father of Svipdag, Beygad and Hvitserk, 14; has dream warning him that Svipdag is in trouble in battle, sends Beygad and Hvitserk to help him, 14; praises King Hrolf to his sons, 15.

SVIPDAG: son of farmer Svip, 14; joins Adils' retinue, 14; does battle with berserkers, 14; leaves Adils, who has abandoned him in battle, to seek a better king, 14; joins King Hrolf in Denmark, 15; mentioned, 16; in Hrolf's retinue, 24; with Hrolf in Adils' hall, 27; warns that Adils is likely to be treacherous, 27; asks Adils for truce for Hrolf, 27; flings fire-stoker into flames in Adils' hall, 28; wants to test if Hrani was Odin, 30; warned by Hjalti of attack by Hjorvard and Skuld, 32.

SWEDEN: ruled by Adils, 11; Svip lives in Sweden, 14; Svipdag leaves Sweden, 15; Hrolf sends men to Sweden to meet Queen Yrsa, 15.

SWEDES: ruled by Adils, 29, 39.

THORIR HOUND'S FOOT: son of Bjorn and Bera, 20; born with dog's feet, 20; draws from rock an axe left him by his father, 21; visits his brother Elk-Frodi, 21; becomes king of the Gauts, 21; mentioned, 22; Bodvar visits him, 23; avenges Bodvar, 34.

UPPDALES: Hring, King of Uppdales in Norway, 17.

UPPSALA: Adils' capital in Sweden, 11, 12, 25, 26, 30.

VALHALLA: Odin's hall, where he receives dead warriors, 33; Hjalti expects to be entertained in Valhalla on the evening after the battle, 33.

VALSLEYT: a jarl, marries Bera, 22.

VAR: the name of King Frodi's two smiths, 3; Regin warns Frodi to be 'wary' in punning song on names of two smiths, 4.

VIFIL: island-dweller skilled in magic, 1; conceals Helgi and Hroar from Frodi, 2; seeress reveals that Hopp and Ho on Vifil's island were Hroar and Helgi, 3.

VOGG: gives Hrolf the name *kraki*, 28; promises to avenge Hrolf's death, 28; warns Hrolf that Adils is sending a monstrous boar against him, 28; rewarded for his help by Hrolf, 29; leads army to avenge Hrolf, 34.

VOTT, 'the Arrogant': one of Hrolf's champions, 32.

YRSA: daughter of Olof by Helgi, 7; Helgi marries Yrsa, not knowing her parentage, 7; has son Hrolf by Helgi, 9; Olof tells her that Helgi is her father and her marriage is incestuous, 10; Yrsa leaves Helgi and returns to Saxland with Olof, 10; marries Adils, although she expects it to turn out badly, 11; welcomes Helgi at Uppsala, not knowing that Adils plans to betray him, 12; reproaches Adils for killing Helgi, 13; urges Adils to take Svipdag into his following, 14; Hrolf appeals to her to help him get the treasure which belonged to Helgi, now held by Adils, 15; mentioned, 16; welcomes and aids Hrolf, 28; reproaches Adils, 28; gives Hrolf Adils' treasures, including ring Sviagris, 29; aids those who avenge Hrolf and his champions, 34.

# READ MORE IN PENGUIN

In every corner of the world, on every subject under the sun, Penguin represents quality and variety – the very best in publishing today.

For complete information about books available from Penguin – including Puffins, Penguin Classics and Arkana – and how to order them, write to us at the appropriate address below. Please note that for copyright reasons the selection of books varies from country to country.

**In the United Kingdom:** Please write to *Dept. EP, Penguin Books Ltd, Bath Road, Harmondsworth, West Drayton, Middlesex UB7 0DA*

**In the United States:** Please write to *Consumer Services, Penguin Putnam Inc., 405 Murray Hill Parkway, East Rutherford, New Jersey 07073-2136.* VISA and MasterCard holders call 1-800-631-8571 to order Penguin titles

**In Canada:** Please write to *Penguin Books Canada Ltd, 10 Alcorn Avenue, Suite 300, Toronto, Ontario M4V 3B2*

**In Australia:** Please write to *Penguin Books Australia Ltd, 487 Maroondah Highway, Ringwood, Victoria 3134*

**In New Zealand:** Please write to *Penguin Books (NZ) Ltd, Private Bag 102902, North Shore Mail Centre, Auckland 10*

**In India:** Please write to *Penguin Books India Pvt Ltd, 11 Community Centre, Panchsheel Park, New Delhi 110017*

**In the Netherlands:** Please write to *Penguin Books Netherlands bv, Postbus 3507, NL-1001 AH Amsterdam*

**In Germany:** Please write to *Penguin Books Deutschland GmbH, Metzlerstrasse 26, 60594 Frankfurt am Main*

**In Spain:** Please write to *Penguin Books S. A., Bravo Murillo 19, 1°B, 28015 Madrid*

**In Italy:** Please write to *Penguin Italia s.r.l., Via Vittorio Emanuele 45/a, 20094 Corsico, Milano*

**In France:** Please write to *Penguin France, 12, Rue Prosper Ferradou, 31700 Blagnac*

**In Japan:** Please write to *Penguin Books Japan Ltd, Iidabashi KM-Bldg, 2-23-9 Koraku, Bunkyo-Ku, Tokyo 112-0004*

**In South Africa:** Please write to *Penguin Books South Africa (Pty) Ltd, P.O. Box 751093, Gardenview, 2047 Johannesburg*

# READ MORE IN PENGUIN

## A CHOICE OF CLASSICS

| | |
|---|---|
| Basho | **The Narrow Road to the Deep North** |
| | **On Love and Barley** |
| Cao Xueqin | **The Story of the Stone** also known as **The Dream of The Red Chamber** (in five volumes) |
| Confucius | **The Analects** |
| Khayyam | **The Ruba'iyat of Omar Khayyam** |
| Lao Tzu | **Tao Te Ching** |
| Li Po/Tu Fu | **Poems** |
| Shikibu Murasaki | **The Tale of Genji** |
| Sarma | **The Pancatantra** |
| Sei Shonagon | **The Pillow Book of Sei Shonagon** |
| Somadeva | **Tales from the Kathasaritsagara** |
| Wu Ch'Eng-En | **Monkey** |

ANTHOLOGIES AND ANONYMOUS WORKS

**The Bhagavad Gita**
**Buddhist Scriptures**
**Chinese Love Poetry**
**The Dhammapada**
**Hindu Myths**
**Japanese No Dramas**
**The Koran**
**The Laws of Manu**
**Poems from the Sanskrit**
**Poems of the Late T'Ang**
**The Rig Veda**
**Speaking of Siva**
**Tales from the Thousand and One Nights**
**The Upanishads**

# READ MORE IN PENGUIN

## A CHOICE OF CLASSICS

| | |
|---|---|
| Adomnan of Iona | **Life of St Columba** |
| St Anselm | **The Prayers and Meditations** |
| Thomas Aquinas | **Selected Writings** |
| St Augustine | **Confessions** |
| | **The City of God** |
| Bede | **Ecclesiastical History of the English People** |
| Geoffrey Chaucer | **The Canterbury Tales** |
| | **Love Visions** |
| | **Troilus and Criseyde** |
| Marie de France | **The Lais of Marie de France** |
| Jean Froissart | **The Chronicles** |
| Geoffrey of Monmouth | **The History of the Kings of Britain** |
| Gerald of Wales | **History and Topography of Ireland** |
| | **The Journey through Wales and The Description of Wales** |
| Gregory of Tours | **The History of the Franks** |
| Robert Henryson | **The Testament of Cresseid and Other Poems** |
| Robert Henryson/ William Dunbar | **Selected Poems** |
| Walter Hilton | **The Ladder of Perfection** |
| St Ignatius | **Personal Writings** |
| Julian of Norwich | **Revelations of Divine Love** |
| Thomas à Kempis | **The Imitation of Christ** |
| William Langland | **Piers the Ploughman** |
| Sir Thomas Malory | **Le Morte d'Arthur** (in two volumes) |
| Sir John Mandeville | **The Travels of Sir John Mandeville** |
| Marguerite de Navarre | **The Heptameron** |
| Christine de Pisan | **The Treasure of the City of Ladies** |
| Chrétien de Troyes | **Arthurian Romances** |
| Marco Polo | **The Travels** |
| Richard Rolle | **The Fire of Love** |
| François Villon | **Selected Poems** |
| Jacobus de Voragine | **The Golden Legend** |

# READ MORE IN PENGUIN

## A CHOICE OF CLASSICS

ANTHOLOGIES AND ANONYMOUS WORKS

**The Age of Bede**
**Alfred the Great**
**Beowulf**
**A Celtic Miscellany**
**The Cloud of Unknowing and Other Works**
**The Death of King Arthur**
**The Earliest English Poems**
**Early Christian Lives**
**Early Irish Myths and Sagas**
**Egil's Saga**
**English Mystery Plays**
**The Exeter Book of Riddles**
**Eyrbyggja Saga**
**Hrafnkel's Saga and Other Stories**
**The Letters of Abelard and Heloise**
**Medieval English Lyrics**
**Medieval English Verse**
**Njal's Saga**
**The Orkneyinga Saga**
**Roman Poets of the Early Empire**
**The Saga of King Hrolf Kraki**
**Seven Viking Romances**
**Sir Gawain and the Green Knight**